FORT HOGAN

**Center Point
Large Print**

**This Large Print Book carries the
Seal of Approval of N.A.V.H.**

FORT HOGAN

Frank Bonham

CENTER POINT PUBLISHING
THORNDIKE, MAINE

This Center Point Large Print edition
is published in the year 2007 by arrangement with
Golden West Literary Agency.

Copyright © 1981 by Frank Bonham.

The text of this Large Print edition is unabridged. In other
aspects, this book may vary from the original edition. Printed in
Thailand. Set in 16-point Times New Roman type.

ISBN-10: 1-58547-981-0
ISBN-13: 978-1-58547-981-8

Library of Congress Cataloging-in-Publication Data

Bonham, Frank.
    Fort Hogan / Frank Bonham.--Center Point large print ed.
        p. cm.
    ISBN-13: 978-1-58547-981-8 (lib. bdg. : alk. paper)
    1. Large type books. I. Title.

PS3503.O4315F67 2007
813'.54--dc22

2006101768

1

EVERY NOW AND THEN Fidel's partner would stuff a few things in a valise and announce that he was taking the afternoon train down to Villa Camargo, Sonora. He was going to scare up some cows for their next buying trip; he would be back in a couple of days. Then he would buckle on a gun, put a blanket roll over his shoulder, and saunter over to the train station.

So far, so good.

But what was to prevent Johnny Hogan from getting off the train on the Mexican side of the international line, a hundred yards from here, and riding back after dark? Absolutely nothing. And he was just the kind of crazy, irresponsible fool who might do it. It was a piss-poor way to feel about a partner, but Gary Fidel had never had any illusions about Hogan, and he had worked too hard setting up the little export-import company he called the Great Western Trading Company to let a wandering roisterer steal from him almost the only item of value in the firm.

So today, near dusk on a blistering July day, with Johnny long gone, he buckled on his Army Colt, rented a horse, and headed northeast up the road to see how Great Western's assets were doing.

On a fresh horse the cache was about an hour's ride from Nogales, A. T. A rose-gray light was settling over the gritty hills around Nogales as he passed through

5

them. The huge, oak-sized mesquites along the river were of a dried-moss color; the graze was high, the color of bedding straw. Fidel heard the bold two-note call of a meadowlark, which seemed to be demanding a response. Won't bother you if you don't bother me, he thought. Can't speak for Hogan, though, and he may be along pretty soon. He'd shoot out a meadow-lark's eye and brag about it.

The horse had the easiest jog in the Territory. A mare, she was a buckskin he often rented. The evening was pleasant, but soon he was brooding again over the problems of smuggling contraband into the sierras of northern Sonora. He had become obsessed with the difficulties. He drew maps and pictures, invented innocent-looking crates and barrels that held arms under layers of mining equipment or corn meal. But nothing seemed feasible.

Fidel's background was primarily mining. Hogan's was gambling and drinking, but he also knew cattle. When Fidel took a railroad shipment of mining equip-ment down to the Villa Camargo siding, where he shifted to wagons, Johnny Hogan would go along with two or three cowhands and buy cattle from a couple of ranches there. Nogales was thronged with cattle buyers, and for a couple of dollars profit per head, they would bring back a hundred steers. In Mexico, they would pay for the cattle with Fidel's profit from the mining supplies. After they had sold the cattle in Nogales, they would divide the take.

They had been doing this for nine months, and Fidel

still had not put together a scheme for moving their main asset from the hills north of Nogales into the Sierra Tipic.

It was almost dark when he reached a pass through some snaglike hills where the railroad began to climb. In the dying light he could still make out red and green mineral stains on the sheer hillsides. Ought to be metal in there, even some gold. But prospectors had burrowed through it all like gophers. He saw a certain distinctive telegraph pole with a crooked crossbar, and began looking for the trail.

When he saw it, he dismounted and tightened the cinch for the climb. Then he stood with one hand on the saddlehorn and listened like a fox. A breeze blew warm and steady, and the ocotillos stood rigid against it. He could hear the wind in the telegraph wires. An owl glided overhead, making no sound at all. The horse shifted its weight and the saddle creaked. But no sounds came to disturb him.

Fidel rode on, along a rocky hillside and into an arroyo that climbed into the hills. He passed some rusting machinery and a stope where a mine had been worked long ago. His memory had to fill in some of what he saw, since it was almost dark now. The stable horse acted as though it had been here before, and Fidel grew suspicious. Had John Hogan rented it, too, for a trip to the mine? The mare started to turn in on a shelf where there was a mine ruin. It had been here, damnit! He kept it moving up canyon for another hundred yards. Then he dismounted and led it into a covey of oaks. He slipped a lead-rope around its neck and tied it to a branch.

From a saddle-bag, he pulled a mine-lamp he had used when he was working in other people's mines. He shoved the handle of a claw-hammer under his belt. He started back, stopping every hundred feet to listen. But would Hogan really do a thing like that? he asked himself. He was too lazy. Crazy enough, maybe, but what would he do with it if he stole it back? Hogan had been lucky to find someone like Fidel, who had had to be a little crazy himself to think he could smuggle it into Mexico.

He made his way carefully to the old mine entrance, and listened again, his hand on his Colt. He struck a match and lit the lamp, flashed the beam over the slightly skewed adit, studied the ground for snakes and evidence of intruders. The weeds, which petered out at the sill, appeared undisturbed. He picked up a stick to use on snakes. He shot the beam around some more, thinking of bats. He hated bats. He had known a miner who died from the bite of a hydrophobia bat.

Painstakingly, he made his way down the tunnel. This was an old-style mine without even any rails. Rubble made the going hard. He came to a point where the hanging-wall of the tunnel sloped down to the floor; the metal had given out here. But the miner had continued smelling for it on the right, where another drift slanted away.

Fidel swung the light there, and drew a relieved breath. A crate, about four and one-half feet long, lay in the rubble. He moved forward, poking the stick around for snakes. Satisfied, he tossed the stick to the floor.

An instant later he yelled, dropped the lamp, and drew his revolver. Black shapes were dropping from a beam and flying into his face. He fell to one knee and fired. The sound deafened and shocked him and brought himself to his senses. The bats flew past him, wings brushing his hair, on down the tunnel. He threshed his arms.

His heart pounded. Still burning, the lamp illuminated the timber where the bats had clung like plums. His heart plunged along like a steam engine. His ears rang. It would be a week before he could hear normally again. He decided he had not been bitten. He sat with his back against the wall a moment, recovering.

In the harsh light, he could read the words stamped on the side of the case.

National Armory, Springfield, Mass.

Gatling Gun, Calibre .45.

Talking to himself about his womanly fears, he drew the hammer from his belt and checked the crate. It had been opened, but apparently only when he had inspected the gun the first time. He inserted the iron claw into the same scars and worked one of the boards loose. Perhaps I do him wrong, he thought; but the crate could still be full of rocks, for which the Yaquis would not pay much.

In the light of the mine-lamp, under a gleaming skin of cosmoline, shone the blued casing of the gun. His eye ran along it, from cascabel plate to front sight, a sturdy weapon like a small cannon, but with ten barrels under the casing. One or two guns like this had been used against the Yaquis by the Mexican Army, but the Yaquis had never been able to capture one. They were willing to pay eight thousand dollars in stolen Mexican Army gold for one, if it were properly adjusted and someone would explain the serving of the weapon to their gunsmith, in Cáhita, the Yaqui tongue.

Fidel had such a man, but the man did not know it yet; and he had the gun. But it was worthless here. The Indians needed the weapon; he needed the money. It was frustrating. The gun, in its case, weighed nearly two hundred pounds. Hogan had made it clear that he wanted no part of the smuggling operation. And Fidel did not really want a lunatic like him around when he attempted to deliver it anyway. So for the time being, the gun, with its enormous firepower—four hundred rounds a minute—would have to remain in the mine like an elusive lode in the stone.

In the meantime, he was relieved to know that Johnny Hogan was either too lazy or too honest to steal back the gun with which he had bought a half-interest in Great Western Trading Company.

10

2

ON A HOT MORNING a few days later, Fidel was reading a Mexican newspaper from Nogales, Sonora, a block from his office. His Benjamin Franklin half-lenses rode the tip of his nose. They were out of place on his brown, mustachioed face, but although he could make out what an eagle was carrying at a mile, he had difficulty with print.

He was sitting at a dusty desk in his one-room office, the lazy morning traffic of the border drifting past the door. Johnny Hogan sat at his own empty desk chewing on a matchstick as he gazed out the door, appearing vaguely bothered. He was a big man of thirty with a clipped chestnut beard, there were brown streaks of gold in it and it shone from regular shampooing.

Without looking at him, Gary Fidel knew he was thinking about his first drink, and that he was bothered because he knew Fidel would say something if he had it before eleven o'clock.

"Not on company time, pardner," he would joke. But he meant it. Fidel knew that what troubled him most of all was that he let anybody else's opinion affect him in any way. He was a free spender, thinker, and drinker. But Fidel was able to get under his skin and keep him from fooling around during the day, when there was often a little work to do. Hogan was probably the laziest mortal alive.

With a pen-knife, Fidel clipped the story he had been reading. "Valverde is putting another army together," he said. "He'll move up the Yaqui River as soon as the weather cools."

"Are you going to stop him?" Hogan yawned.

"You'd think they'd have had a belly-full of Indians by now," said Fidel. "Hundreds of years of fighting Yaquis, two armies wiped out in the last three years. But they're still riding into the mountains to get themselves ambushed."

"You part Mexican?" Hogan asked, curiously.

It was odd, Fidel thought, that he had never asked that before. "Basque," he said. "I come from a long line of Oregon sheepherders. But Fidel is a Spanish word. It means faithful."

"Like a hound dog," Hogan smiled. "Arf, arf." He produced a pocket watch and wound it. It was a heavy gold timepiece. He also wore three gold rings and a gold bracelet with the Mexican eagle on it. He craved gold the way children craved candy. The jewelry also gave him a cash reserve when he ran out of money during an evening of gambling.

"You part gypsy?" Fidel asked him, with a smirk.

Hogan blinked. "Me? What makes you think so?"

"All the gold bangles. And the wandering."

"I don't know what I am," Hogan said, "except that whatever I am, I'm a hundred percent."

"That's for damn sure," Fidel said, with a laugh. He filed the newspaper story in a pigeon-hole. "Of course," he said, going back to his obsession, "the war

12

gets renewed every few years. A new governor is appointed in Sonora, and the President presents him with the Yaqui River Valley, the fertilest thing this side of a sixteen-year-old girl. All he's got to do is take it. Then Diaz will take it from the Governor." He was talking to himself, but using John's ears.

"Speaking of girls," said Hogan, reflectively, "did it ever strike you that there's something fishy about my landlady?"

"No, not at all," Fidel said tartly. "What's fishy about her?" He wondered if Hogan had figured out that he was purely crazy about Allie.

Hogan clawed at his beard. In hot weather it itched. Nogales was the wrong town for beard-lovers. *"Número uno,"* he said, "she's still in mourning, keeps Bibles on all the tables, but doesn't go to church. That's fishy."

"Good point."

"Número dos, my sister wrote a better hand at twelve than Allie does at twenty-whatever-she-is. I mail letters for her sometimes, and they all look like Minnie's letter to Santa Claus. And every single one of them goes to San Francisco."

The handwriting, too, was an interesting point, and one that Fidel had pondered. Why did the young widow of a French mining engineer, who read poetry, cooked like a saint, and knew all the subtler tricks of coquetry, sometimes give the impression that she was eleven or twelve years old?

"And another thing. This is rare!" said Hogan. "All

13

the women she writes to are named after birds: Phoebe, Robin, Piper. All of them!"

"Hmm," said Fidel. Now that was really interesting! A code? Robin: *"I need money."* Phoebe: *"Do you need money?"*

"What do you reckon she's up to?" he asked his partner. His brown eyes were intent. Anything about Allie Denis fascinated and excited him. She was a woman in a million. Would she never finish mourning for that old Frenchman?

She and her husband had lived here a couple of years, although he was down at the mines in Sonora most of the time. Allie had helped take care of old Doctor Hall during his last illness, and after his death—before his son, Tom, came home from the Army—she had rented the big house from him and started taking in boarders.

"I don't think she's up to anything," Hogan said slowly. "I just can't dope her out. It's like she was born the day she married Monsoor Bernard Denis. 'Bare-nar and I were at Nevada City for two years. Bare-nar thought of opening a restaurant, so we wouldn't have to live in no more mining camps.' That's what she said. Then she catches herself and says, '*Any* more, excuse me.' Shit, I don't care about her grammar, if she'd just take off her clothes."

"Watch your mouth, John," Fidel said sharply. "You're not talking about a hurdy-gurdy girl."

"Well, wash my mouth out with bourbon, pardner," Hogan laughed. His smile was a cocky leer. It went

14

with the fact that his right eye was slightly smaller, so that he had a perpetual look of skepticism.

"She's only been widowed a year," Fidel said sternly. "Maybe she loved the man. She must take her mourning seriously. That's why she won't rent me a room—she likes me too much. Can you imagine any other reason a woman would trust you more than me?"

Hogan laughed and began cleaning his nails with a gold pen-knife. He roomed at Allie's.

"Another thing," he said. "How-come all the people she writes to are women? Doesn't she have any uncles, or a father or something? Try finding *that* out, if you think wrestling a trout is slippery."

"Have you seen that Yaqui drum at her place?" Fidel asked. "Belonged to Tom Hall's father. Doctor Hall told me once he took the boy into the Yaqui country one time, and they inducted him into the fox-soldier society. You've got to admire those bastards," he said fiercely. "One fight, all fight—men, women, and children."

Hogan spat out the match and got up, closed the knife and dropped it in his pocket. "You and your pissant Yaquis. You'll either get scalped by them, or stood up before a Mexican firing squad. I hate to think how much blasting powder we allegedly sold to the mines that you handed off to the Yaquis. Leave me out of your smuggling, amigo. I'll handle the cattle end of it." He yawned and looked out the door.

"Going out?" Fidel asked.

"*Sí, compadre.* Okay by you?"

"Where?"

"Down the street, damn it!"

"Why don't you go up the street, to the bank? Here—I'll write the check. But don't cash it until this afternoon, when I need the money. *Claro?*"

He opened a large check book and wrote a draft for forty-three hundred dollars. On the stub, he wrote, *Mining machinery.*

"What am I supposed to do with this?"

"The freight should have been here on last night's train. I'm going over and wire El Paso to make sure it's on the way. Those Mexican miners want service, and it's all we can give them that a bigger outfit can't. But make sure we get the money out before they close, John, so we can start unloading my machinery tonight."

"Our machinery," said Hogan, who had no idea what they were buying. "Why don't I just get the money out now?"

Fidel laughed. "What a question. If there were no saloons and no girls and no roulette wheels in Nogales, I might think it was a good idea."

Hogan put on a high-crowned sombrero with gold stars on the band. It was Mexican, as were his blond, stitched boots. He was very vain of his small feet. Fidel sniffed as he passed. He always smelled very interesting, a musk compounded of bay rum, tobacco, a slight odor of perspiration, and whiskey. Possibly an exciting odor, to a woman. To Fidel it seemed a bit indecent.

16

"You coming?" Hogan asked.

"I'm going to write the telegram first. I'll lock up."

He found the address of the El Paso firm and started on the telegram. There were letters, papers, account books, and a clock on his desk; nothing but tobacco and curios in Hogan's. Each man kept his own books, though Hogan kept his on the backs of envelopes.

Fidel had accumulated a few hundred dollars in the nine months they had been partners, and Johnny Hogan had had some memorable evenings on both sides of the line, the Ambos Nogales. Fidel lived in a room at the Montezuma Hotel, among mining men and cattle buyers from all over hell's half-acre, while lucky John Hogan boarded at Allie's.

Fidel put his head out the door and looked up and down the road. The unpaved street curved gently east, ramshackle but self-consciously modern, with its cob-webs of telephone wires. On the walks there were women with parasols, buggies with umbrellas in the road. The street curled through a shallow pass in the desert hills. A half-block north he saw John talking to a hurdy-gurdy girl, his palms against the wall behind her, imprisoning her. She was laughing.

Fidel went back and took an Army revolver from a desk drawer. With a small screw driver, he removed the cedar buttplates and then the backstrap and trigger-guard assembly, leaving the hammer mecha-nism exposed. Using a small file, he blunted the edge of the cocking sear. Then he reassembled the gun. The

17

hammer could now be forced off cocking position.

He shoved the gun into a holster, but left the belt in the drawer. Then he ran down the roller of his desk and locked it. It helped keep John and the dust out.

3

TRADE HAD BEEN MOVING through the pass in the brushy hills for centuries. Northbound or southbound, it crept through the funnel called Nogales. The railroad went along one side of the pass, carrying freight to the Sonoran capital of Hermosillo and the port of Guaymas, and hauling cattle and mineral products north. There were fifteen thousand miners in Cananea, Sonora, alone, and thousands more in the mountains further south. Fidel traded with the smaller outfits in the mountains.

He thought out the telegram as he followed the crooked telephone and electric poles to the station on Morley Avenue. He had to decide on a plan of action with the telegrapher, who was Tom Hall; Fidel needed him badly. A hot wind was blowing through the station. Fidel could feel the grit on his teeth. He walked around to the platform and looked at a line of dusty hopper cars resting on a siding. Water towers rose beyond them, dripping alkali water into the mud at their bases.

He entered the telegraph office and leaned on the counter, watching Hall take down a message coming through his nickel-plated key. Hall looked up, continuing to write.

"Hello, Fidel," he said. He was a slender, neatly-dressed man of about twenty-five with a light brown mustache and hair parted on one side. He wore a striped shirt and vest, across which swung his father's gold watch-chain. He was also wearing a diamond ring Fidel had seen on Doctor Hall's hand.

"How do you do that?" Fidel asked him.

"Do what?"

"Talk and take down a message at the same time."

Hall smiled his almost apologetic smile. "Just something you learn. Habit."

"Remarkable," Fidel said. "Here—I'll write down a message I want to send."

The key went silent, and Hall wrote something on a message pad. He opened a door and called,

"Hilario!"

An old man with a brown face and white mustache came to the door. Hall spoke to him in Spanish, and the man carried the message away.

"Now, then. What've you got?"

"This goes to Lone Star Mining and Supply, El Paso."

Hall figured the charges. He was quiet, and if he had any emotions he always managed to hide them. That was one thing that concerned Fidel: he could not figure him out. And how could you go into business with someone you couldn't figure out? At least he understood Johnny. He also understood that he very much needed Tom Hall.

He paid him for the wire, but lingered. "I'll wait," he said.

"There won't be an answer for an hour or so," Hall said. "But suit yourself."

He sat down again and transmitted the message. Fidel wiped the film of perspiration from his forehead. He pulled the Colt from his belt then and laid it on the counter. Immediately, Hall showed interest.

"What've you got?" he asked.

"Old single-action Colt," Fidel said. "Look at this. Damn' thing's a menace. Won't stay on full cock if it's dropped."

Hall winced. "I wouldn't make a practice of dropping cocked guns, anyway. Lemme see it."

He drew the gun from the holster and did some gunman twirls with it before settling down to inspecting it, after first making sure it was unloaded. His hand was quick and clever.

"The sear's gone," he said. "You need a new hammer. Take it up to Bob Eldred's. Shouldn't cost over a dollar."

"How can you tell without looking?"

Hall worked the hammer. "I can see right through those buttplates. I'd like to have a dime for all the single-action Colts I've serviced."

"Not much ever goes wrong with them, I'll say that. This is a 'seventy-four model. Had it for—"

"Seventy-three," Hall said, so mildy that his correction could not have been resented.

"I see. You were in Signal Corps, weren't you?" Fidel asked.

"The last year and a half. Two and a half years in Ordnance."

20

"Ah. Why'd you change?"

"Their idea. I was lucky they didn't assign me to Medical Corps because my father was a doctor."

"He was a fine man," Fidel said. "Treated a broken thumb for me last year. I sent you a card of condolence."

"Thank you. I got so many of them I couldn't answer many."

"I wish you could do the work for me, Tom," Fidel said earnestly. "I've got more confidence in you. Eldred horsed around with my Henry rifle for a month and then said he couldn't get the part."

"Well, he's—he ought to retire. But I can understand," Hall said. "Don't pass this on, but I made him an offer. I'd like to open a gun-shop, but I don't want to compete with him. There's as much gun work as any one man can handle. He more or less turned me down, though. So I'll wait and see. . . ."

"What other kinds of guns did you work on?" Fidel asked. "What's your specialty?"

"My specialty is anything with a barrel and a hammer. I worked on everything we had, even a Gatling gun."

Fidel's nerves seemed to throb like guitar strings. "Is that right? You don't see many of them around, do you?"

"No." Hall holstered the trader's Colt and thought for a moment. "I'll fix it for you," he said. "I've got my own tools, and a few parts. Don't tell anybody."

"That's great, Tom. I don't suppose you've got any nice grips? Ivory, or something?"

"I could find something across the line. There's a beautiful set of silver plates—how high do you want to go?"

"I'd go fifteen or twenty."

"I'll find you something."

"Muy bien, amigo."

"Ah, you espeak Espanish!" said Hall.

"Sure do. Somebody told me you speak Cáhita. Is that what you call it?"

"Yaqui? Yes. We had a Yaqui handyman who drove my father's buggy so he could sleep on night calls, and I had a Yaqui wet-nurse, so I guess I come by it honestly."

"Interesting. Listen, I'm going up to Allie's place for lunch—I take most of my meals there. What time do you get off?"

"I'll shut down for lunch at twelve. I guess she could find another plate for me. I'll lock your gun in my desk."

4

FIDEL LABORED OVER THE books in the suffocating office, the half-lenses slipping down his sweaty nose. He had rolled up his sleeves in order to think better. He still had some of the ways of a laborer, and the laborer's fear of that which was worse than death: assassination by debt.

He listed every possible asset of the Great Western Trading Company on a sheet of ledger paper. The total was humiliating. The most tangible asset of all was the mystery which must not even be whispered. Beyond the tangible assets, however, he had some intangible ones he tried to express when he made a new loan at the bank; the same ones he was trying to make young Hall smell on him: his vigor, intelligence, and ambition.

He wiped the steel nib on a penwiper and folded the sheet of paper, closed the desk again and locked it. There was nothing of special value in it, but he figured that the less John knew about his personal business, the better.

He locked the office and went to his hotel to wash up. The lobby smelled of dust and cigars, and buzzed like a beehive. The Montezuma Hotel was home to dozens of cattle buyers and mining promoters, here to bid on Mexican cattle and mining properties on both sides of the border. There was laughter, loud talk, and whispered secrets.

In his room, he stripped off his sweat-ringed shirt, washed up, and carefully combed his hair, parting it in the middle. He brushed his brown mustache with his hairbrush and looked at himself skeptically. Was he beginning to appear middle-aged? He was only thirty-two; but that was old to be getting started. Some of the years he had put into labor showed in little scars on his face and hands, and in small lines, hardly deeper than the scratches in silverware, around his eyes. There was a white half-moon in the brown skin of his chin, a scar in each eyebrow.

Under the hot, hazy sky, he walked up the hill to Allie Denis's boarding house.

The house was on a hill a block west of the main street, high enough that it looked out over the mud-colored town and the railroad station. A smoky, pearl-gray sky, with dull layers of cloud, lay over the hills. A haze of dust drifted along Arroyo Street. He stopped behind a low rock wall, lifted his gray Stetson and wiped his brow, already perspiring again. There were black-branched fruit trees beside the house, a wind-mill spinning behind it. On the long gallery sat two old men, Allie's boarders. One was Henry Montana, a druggist; the other was Arthur Cleaveland, a retired bookkeeper.

Arthur always called Fidel, Mister; it was part of his training. He was a born subordinate, and an asthmatic. It seemed to Fidel they often went together.

"Good day, Mr. Fidel," he said. "Sit down, rest your-self."

Fidel let himself into a rawhide chair beside the wheezing old man in his undertaker's suit and boiled collar. "What do I have to do to get you to call me Gary?" he asked.

"In good time, Mr. Fidel," said Arthur pleasantly. He looked like a baby parrot, with his skinny neck, bald skull, and large nose. On a map, navigators would refer to such a protuberance as Arthur's Nose.

"What's new, Henry?" Fidel said to the druggist.

Henry Montana was a middle-aged man with a yellow-brown face, lined and rather jaded. His

24

looped hound's-eyes always looked disappointed.

"I'll tell you boys a secret," he said, lowering his voice. "There are more dope-fiends in this town than you'd believe possible. Scratch a lunger, and you uncover a dope-fiend."

Arthur frowned at him, shocked. "Oh, Mr. Montana, you can't mean that."

"Mrs. Winslow's Soothing Syrup," whispered the druggist, nodding. "It *ought* to soothe a person—it's laced with morphine, a habit-forming drug! We've got more than our share of lungers, of course, and they're all taking Mrs. Winslow's, or one of the catarrh powders, which are largely a substance called cocaine. I have people using a bottle of Mrs. Winslow's a day! And not all lungers," he hinted.

"Meaning no offense, Mr. Montana," wheezed Arthur, "but I hope I never see the day I'm sick enough to need any of your medicine. Once you start, you're a goner."

Henry winked at Fidel. "You'd be a lot better off if you smoked Asthmador, Mr. Cleaveland. But I was telling Dr. Noon yesterday, they ought to have some kind of control over drugs like morphine and cocaine."

"I agree," said Arthur. Fidel saw that he was bursting with the need to talk numbers. He had never had a wife, but there had been lovely numbers in his life; stacks of figures drawn as lovingly as a jeweler's engraving; mopterious signs and symbols. Having nothing better to do, he did Fidel's bookkeeping, and

25

was always organizing studies of his operation. He worried about Fidel.

"Mr. Fidel," he said, "I've done a new analysis of your shipping costs. It—it shocks me, really. You'd save six percent—actually, nearly seven—if you could find a way to order full carloads instead of fractional loads. A full load can go into Sonora without the necessity of unloading and reloading. Each movement of freight costs money—"

"I do it when I can," Fidel said. "If I had the capital to buy ahead—"

"The poor get poorer, and the rich get richer," said Mr. Montana.

Arthur looked at him in disapproval. "I think it would be more apt to say that it takes money to make money. Mr. Fidel is not poor."

"He's not rich either," said Montana with a wink.

Arthur coughed, dabbing at his lips with a wadded handkerchief. "And then there is the matter of mule and wagon rental. I think you would be better off to ship your wagon and span of mules south, and board them permanently at Camargo, where you unload your freight. As I see it, you seldom need a wagon here in town. Yet you have to pay daily board on the mules, and storage on the wagon. You'd be better off renting an outfit here when you need it. And then you wouldn't need to rent one in Sonora."

"That's a point," Fidel agreed. "But sometimes I have to haul heavy supplies from Proto Brothers to the railroad station."

"If you paid a little extra, they'd deliver for you," said the old man, earnestly.

"True. But the wagon's too light for most of my work down there. The road from Camargo is terrible, coming and going."

Arthur frowned. "I see. . . . Wouldn't it be the same going as coming?"

"No, because I make a triangle. Due east to La Ventana, then back southwest to Rincon. I usually leave some supplies at the village there, barrels of meal, for instance, and salt pork. Then back to the railroad at Villa Camargo on the other leg of the triangle."

"Barrels? Have you asked yourself whether it might not be better to go to Rincon first, rather that to La Ventana? You'd be dropping off some of your heaviest freight, which would give you a faster trip from there on."

Fidel nodded. He had always made the triangle in the same fashion as he had done it the first time. "I'll give you the mileage and tonnage on it. Maybe you can do a study on it for me. I'm like the mules, I'll go where you point me."

"And take along an engineer's level, would you? You could do some estimates of the average grade. . . ."

"I'll do that."

"Of course there are always ways a man could get rich," said Arthur, "if he had a little capital."

"Such as?"

Arthur leaned forward. "The hog market! We're paying through the nose—the snout, you might say, ha

27

ha!—to import Mexican lard, soap, and candles. There are few things simpler and cheaper to manufacture than lard, soap, and candles. And the pork is sought after. Labor is cheap, and if you could assure a farmer of a market for his product, you could get the hogs, render the fat for next to nothing—and what is simpler making than soap? As for candles—"

The mosquito-bar door screeched, and Allie Denis looked out. "Mr. Fidel, will you come inside, please?—Dinner will be ready in a few minutes, boys."

The boys murmured. Calling lunch dinner was only one of the continental ideas she had caught from Bernard Denis.

Fidel followed her into the vestibule, which was mellowly lighted by a stained-glass window. A hall ran straight back like a tunnel, the kitchen and three bedrooms opening off it. At the rear was a dark little junction to the bathroom and two other bedrooms. Allie unlocked the door on the left—Johnny Hogan's room—and went inside. She was a very small erect figure in a black silk skirt and black taffeta waist with a high standing collar and full sleeves. In green, red, or any other color, he thought, she would have been a knockout.

Fidel followed her into the room. It was large and clean but the bed had been stripped. Clothing and a small canvas-covered trunk were tumbled on the mattress.

28

"I'd appreciate it," said Allie Denis, "if you'd put *those things* on the chiffonier in this poke and give them to your partner. He knows the rule in this house—no liquor and no women. She must have come and gone through the window."

The things on the chiffonier were a bottle of whiskey, one-third empty, and a red garter. Fidel accepted the paper sack the little woman handed him.

"I'll tell him, Allie, but only if you'll call me by my Christian name. Don't take him out on me."

"All right. I'm sorry. Gary, then. Will you please tell Mr. Hogan that he is to move out after work today?"

Fidel smiled at her. She was built like a cricket, but with a handsome bust and an attractive though slightly monkey-featured face. For some reason he was taken by her sweet, wry features. Her hair was brushed to a small bun on top of her head.

"Come on, Allie. Aren't you playing the hanging judge? He probably brought the garter home from Brickwood's."

"No. There were—other indications. This isn't the first straw, but it's the last. He comes home after twelve, drunk most often, and swears in the bathroom. Then he wakes up with nightmares and disturbs the whole house."

"I'll tell him. Now there'll be room for me, won't there?"

He reached out and tugged at one of the tiny gold crosses she wore in her earlobes. She put her hand on his, but he could see that she was trying not to smile.

"I'm sorry, Gary," she said. "But Mr. Hall asked me to save him the first vacancy, and, after all, it's his house."

"Too bad. Do you know I've lived in company shacks, railroad towns, and hotels all my ad-dult life?"

"Well, why haven't you married and settled down?"

"Living in mining camps, I haven't been tempted. And I didn't want to take a wife into sink-holes like that. Also—the big point—the right one didn't come along."

Allie took the whiskey bottle and garter and stuffed them into the sack Fidel held. "Don't forget to tell John Hogan. There is no bed for him here tonight."

"There have been women who found me attractive, Allie," Fidel said, gravely teasing. "As I find you."

"I'm sure there have. Now I've got to—"

"I'm in a dangerous trade, Allie. A Yaqui might mistake me for a Mexican and shoot me. Or a wagon might turn over on me. Would you want me to die unfulfilled?"

She was looking at the center of his double-breasted shirt. He put his fingertip under her chin and made her look into his eyes. She wore an expression that both daunted and excited him, the most personal expression he had ever seen on her face. She looked vulnerable, excited, yet almost frightened.

"Yes, I know about accidents," she said. "And I don't want to be widowed twice."

"Don't misunderstand me," he said hastily. "I don't let accidents happen. But life is short, Allie, and—"

30

"Please!" she whispered, trying to get past him. He continued to block her.

"Allie, Allie! You're a mystery woman. John and I were talking about it this morning. Things like your dressing like a nun—but never going to church! And as hot as it is, it's always long sleeves. I'd give a lot to see you in a red dress without sleeves."

"Mr. Fidel!" Allie said. "My personal life is—I'd rather not talk about it. I had the greatest respect for my husband. I know you must think that because he was older than me—than I—"

"Come on, Allie," Fidel chuckled. "*I'm* older than you—it isn't that. But how long do you have to wear mourning?"

"Bernard was a man I'll never forget. He brought wonderful things into my life. I won't throw away his memory like flowers that have faded."

"But after they've lost their fragrance—" He got that far when she pushed past him and fled down the hall to the kitchen, as if he were a tormentor. He thought he heard her sob.

My God! he thought. What was so wrong with that? Carrying Hogan's whiskey bottle and red garter, and shaking his head, he went back to the porch.

31

5

ALLIE DENIS SET A fine table. The china, silverware and crystal were elegant, having belonged to Tom Hall's mother. She always managed to have a few flowers, which Fidel sometimes recognized as weeds, but attractive ones, like Indian paintbrush or verbena. As for food, today it was—she announced in French—*haricots verts, poire d'avocat, pommes de terres braisées,* and *poulet à la casserole.* This translated to string beans, alligator pear from Sonora, braised potatoes, and chicken stew.

The only unpopular dish was a salad, which consisted simply of leaves of lettuce torn up like paper and doused with vinegar and oil! An elderly lady boarder named Miss Peacock tried some, but the men were leary of eating such obvious rabbit food, and avoided it. Otherwise it was all delicious, and the men, and Miss Peacock, a teacher on summer vacation, praised her cooking. Fidel noted that even she, a maiden lady, wore a short-sleeved shirtwaist.

"Thank you," Allie said. "My late husband deserves all the credit. He taught me the *cuisine* of his home in Southern France. It's Perigordian."

"Is that something like paregoric?" asked Mr. Montana, the druggist.

"Why, Mr. Montana," Allie chided gently, then laughed.

Fidel did not comment, having heard enough about

Bernard to last him at least through the hot weather.

"Sometime," Allie promised, "we're going to have *escargots*."

"S-cargos?" said old Arthur. "What kind of cargos are those?"

"I won't tell you. It will be a surprise."

Fidel opened the little envelope Tom Hall had brought him from the telegraph office, while the others chatted.

Goods shipped July 11. Arrive afternoon July 12, Lone Star Mining, the telegram read. "That'll be about four o'clock?" Fidel asked Hall.

Hall nodded. He sat at Fidel's left. Fidel knew this was not the time to talk business with Hall, but it would have to be soon. He needed a gunsmith.

"I was talking to a fellow at the hotel today. He's with one of the mines at Oro Blanco," he said.

Everyone waited, and Hall watched him try to handle a drumstick with a knife and fork. Allie made you want to improve your manners.

"And what did he say, Mr. Fidel?" asked Miss Peacock, a gentle lady with a Tennessee accent, and the smooth clear skin of a child.

"Said it will be years before silver comes back, and he recommends gold stock. What do you think, Tom?"

"I don't know. My father was the speculator. He didn't have much luck predicting whether it would be a boy or a girl, they say, but he was pretty good at guessing whether a mine would pay off."

How much did he leave you? Fidel wanted to bawl.

33

"He did as much speculating as doctoring in the last year," he said. "After his stroke."

"So I gather."

Fidel's spirits sank; but then Hall said quietly, "I'm not a gambler, myself. I sold most of the stock he left me. I'll sink it in something else."

While Fidel was planning his next move, Miss Peacock asked: "And where does your business take you this time, Mr. Fidel?"

"Oh—to a town called La Ventana," muttered Fidel, preoccupied with strategy.

Allie looked up quickly.

"Is it dangerous country?" Miss Peacock pursued.

"There's always the chance of bandits, but the Yaqui trouble is farther south." Fidel started when he realized that Allie was blatantly staring at him. Then she looked down at her plate, but quickly looked up at him again.

"My husband is buried at La Ventana," she said.

"Is that so?" he said. "Ever been there?"

"No. . . . Bernard never let me go with him, and I've respected his wishes. I should say, what kinda—sort of community is it?"

Fidel was intrigued; he had touched a nerve. "Fair-sized *ciudad,*" he said. "A part-time river, big empty plaza, mines in all the hills. A nice view from above the town. That's why they call it La Ventana—the window. A church—"

Allie's eyes widened. "You wouldn't know, of course, to what saint the church is dedicated?"

Fidel grinned. "A local miracle-worker called

34

Santa Elena de Arizpe. Died about 1600. Why?"

". . . Just curiosity. My husband was a devout Catholic, and he attended mass there while he was in La Ventana. He died of a heart attack, you know."

Fidel knew. He knew Denis had had a heart attack here, and Doctor Hall, Tom's father, had taken care of him. In a few weeks he had been able to go back to work at La Ventana, where he was an engineer. Then he had died.

He was going to speak to Hall about sending a wire to Villa Camargo, on the railroad, asking a rancher to reserve a wagon and a team of mules for him. But Allie went on quickly while everyone looked at her; all were surprised at the color in her face and her breathless rush of words.

"Would you do something for me while you're in La Ventana?"

"Practically anything." He winked at Miss Peacock.

"I don't know whether you've noticed, but churches have a sort of bulletin board behind certain *santos,* where people pin little silver images of parts of the body. *Milagros,* they're called."

Allie mimicked pinning one up. "They're tokens of gratitude to the saints for helping. A person who is healed of a rheumatic leg might pin up a silver leg, or for headaches it would be a tiny head. Or a silver eye, a foot, or—"

She paused, glancing around the table. Most of them knew it already, and Fidel was surprised that she should explain it.

35

"My husband promised Santa Felicitas, here in town, that if he recovered from his heart attack he would give her a golden heart, not just a silver one. He wrote me from La Ventana that he had bought a lovely one, and was wearing it as an amulet. He'd had it engraved *'Merci, Sta. Felicitas'*."

"Ironic," Miss Peacock said sweetly, "that he should die of a heart seizure while wearing his thanks around his neck." Fidel knew she was a strong Baptist.

"I expect the Mexicans hung it behind one of their own *santos,*" Fidel commented.

"Do you think so?" Allie asked quickly. "I was afraid someone might have stolen it. . . ."

"Might have, but I think they'd be too superstitious—excuse me, religious—to steal it. Do you want me to look for it?"

"Would you? Oh, I'd be so grateful!"

Fidel was charged with envy and hate for the dead Frenchman. "I'll look. Did you want to wear it, or—?"

She had to clear her throat. "I'll hang it in our church. He promised it to Santa Felicitas."

After lunch, Fidel dropped a silver half-dollar in the cut-glass bowl on the sideboard where the casual trade paid for their meals. Hall paid, too. Allie Denis thanked them, then asked Fidel:

"When will you be going?"

"Tomorrow, if today's train's on time. I have to reload to a Mexican flat-car this afternoon, do some

36

paperwork and make my peace with Mexican customs. I'll leave around noon, but I'll talk to you tonight, or before I go."

"Thank you! Oh, and would you post this for me?"

Post. . . . Another affectation she had caught from Bare-nar Denis. "Sure." Walking out, he read the address.

Miss Phoebe Gentry
Post Office Box 1154
San Francisco, California

All spelled out in full, and looking as though a child had written it. Another bird for San Francisco. . . .

Walking down the hill, Fidel said bluntly to Hall:

"I've got a suggestion for you. You've got money to invest. Why don't you buy in with me and Hogan?"

Hall studied him. "Are you serious?"

"Dead serious. With more capital, I could step up my operations. I might even do a little arms dealing, with the Sonorenses, but I'd need a gunsmith to proof the weapons for me."

Hall stroked his blond mustache. "A Sonorense is a person who lives in Sonora. Which color are you talking about?"

"Well, there's not much chance to sell to the Indians."

Hall's cool gaze regarded him sardonically. "Come on, Gary. That's what you're doing, isn't it?"

". . . As a sideline. But it's pitiful what I've been able to do for the Indians. I always carry a couple of bandoliers of ammunition down for them, and leave a

Colt on a rock now and then. My sympathies are with them, sure."

"Mine too; but I don't think I want to get involved in gun-running."

Fidel hesitated. ". . . One gun, of the right kind, could make a hell of a difference in the first battle of the winter. Might turn the tide for a year. I mean something like a Gatling gun. Fire as fast as you can crank it."

"But sensitive as a sandpapered snake," said the telegrapher. "They've got to be tuned like a Swiss watch."

"Was that one of the things you did in the Army?"

Hall nodded. "Sure."

"I've got one," Fidel said. "I don't know how I'll get it down there, but I'll manage somehow. But it won't be of any use to them if it isn't set up right. And I've got to move it knocked down."

"So you need a gunsmith who speaks *Cáhita,*" Hall said.

"You got it, partner," Fidel said quickly.

"I might be willing," Hall said. "but only on my terms. First, I don't want to join your company. Second, I'd go down ahead of time, on some pretext, and just be in the area when you needed me. Just because I sympathize with the Yaquis. But only this one time. Gun-runners don't live as long as I plan to. And they die like dogs."

"One time—agreed. But why not come into the firm?"

Hall's bleached blue eyes regarded him steadily. "Because I don't particularly like your partner. Don't trust him, don't want to be involved with him."

"Our operations are really separate. One of these days, when I've got some cash, I'll buy him out. He's footloose; I've been surprised he's stayed around this long. The gun will sell for eight thousand dollars gold, half to me, half to John. If you come into the firm, I'll give you half of my share."

Hall laughed. "But you'll always be scheming ways to smuggle guns down to the Rio Yaqui. And one fine day you'll be standing with a bandage around your eyes in a plaza somewhere, having a last cigarette. I don't want to be standing beside you."

Fidel shook his head. "No, no! This isn't a career. I want to help them, but mainly I'm helping myself. This is seed money. I need it bad. After I get it—"

He hesitated. For some reason, he very much wanted Hall to understand him. Maybe it was because Hall was a man he did not quite understand himself, a still-waters man, one who had resources in his head as well as the bank. He liked the things he didn't say as well as the things he did. He felt, too, that he might be a good-luck charm, like that amulet Allie wanted him to bring home. "Well, I just think you'd be a good man to have on my side," he said.

"Thanks. We'll talk about it again, sometime."

6

FIDEL UNLOCKED THE OFFICE and took a last breath of
fresh air. He composed a telegram to be sent to the
Mexican railroad stop of Villa Camargo. Camargo
was a *población,* not even a village or a pueblo. At the
foot of a mountain lay a railroad siding, some loading
chutes and holding pens for cattle, a water tower, a
gray mountain of mesquite wood for locomotives, and
a dozen adobe buildings.

His telegrams served a second, secret end: the one-
eyed railroad telegrapher, a Yaqui sympathizer, noti-
fied someone who alerted a Yaqui runner that he
would be bringing a little something—ammunition,
dynamite—whatever he thought he could smuggle in.
In return, they paid in Mexican gold.

At a quarter to two, he went down the street to the
Palace Saloon to look for Hogan. The Palace was the
last building on the east side of the street before the
buffer strip that separated the two nations. The saloon
had a green canvas awning that fended off some of the
blazing sunlight. Fidel entered a musty, resounding
gloom where feeble electric lights winked like mine-
lamps in the smoke. The town had electricity and an
ice-house. It was crowded with men, most of them
from out of town, mining and cattle men; workmen,
promoters, buyers. The men at the bar stood about a
foot from each other and shouted in one another's
face. A lamp swung above a roulette table and a half-

dozen players were seated around it with silver and gold pieces instead of chips. It was a town that believed in metal.

Hogan, at the long bar, saw him and raised his arm. He was with one of his regular hands, Chet Hardin, who worked at a livery stable when Hogan did not need him. Fidel joined them and ordered a beer. It was icy, the way he liked it. He sprinkled some salt on it and watched the creamy head form.

"What do you hear?" Hogan asked, stroking his fine, clipped beard like a fur merchant appraising a pelt. And grinning, with one eye shut. An interesting face, but not one Fidel liked to see on a man he was practically married to. It was too devilish.

"We leave tomorrow," he said. "The freight will be in by four. I'll get some men moving it onto a Mexican car, and then take the invoices over and get things straightened out. Have you got a written order for the cattle?"

Hogan looked at the big gold lion's-head ring on his right hand. "Oh, yes," he said. "A hundred head."

"At how much?"

"Sixteen."

Fidel drank some beer and shook his head. "No, John. We got seventeen last time, and the buyers are still hungry. Did you talk to What's-his-name, from Kansas City—Johnson? I saw him at the hotel."

Hogan shrugged. "The man I made the deal with will put the money in the bank for us the day we come back."

41

"Hell, they all will," said Fidel, impatiently. "Think of it this way, John. We'll pay fourteen dollars a head, cash, at Camargo. The railroad will want some money, and the customs people. And Chet and your other men will have to be paid. So our sixteen hundred begins to look more like one-fifty."

"Hard life," said Chet Hardin. He had a fleshy face with eyes that were swollen slits, with no eyes showing; he looked like a blind man. He was bald, and had probably once been handsome, but booze had remodeled his features. He was all right for loading cattle, but a day in the saddle would have killed him.

"That's the way it goes," Hogan said, irritatingly, with a big smile at Hardin.

"It doesn't have to. I'll look the man up myself."

"I've already got it in writing with Cheyenne Cattle."

"Who's their buyer?" It had never entered his head before that John was clever enough to cheat him. Now he realized he might very easily be taking a little on the side. Hogan paused before saying,

"Guy named Aguirre."

". . . Okay. I'll talk to him. If I can't jack him up, we'll have to cut costs somewhere. Take Chet and one other man down, and we'll hire a couple of men in Mexico."

"Fidel, why don't you open a pawnshop?" said Hogan. "Buy people's old clothes and junk jewelry. Man, I want English-speaking hands, so I don't have to grab a dictionary every time I want to cuss them out."

Hardin chuckled. He took a sip of whiskey and knocked it back with a swallow of beer. "I'd be glad to translate."

"Okay, John," Fidel said. "Your department. Don't let the bank close before you get the money."

"I'll be at the depot at three-thirty. Five dollars says I'm there before the train."

"If I could afford it, I'd bet, because then I'd know you'd be on time for a change."

Hogan grinned and drank a little beer.

"Where can I find Aguirre?" Fidel asked.

"He's over there playing roulette," Hogan said. "The man in the black suit."

Fidel grimaced. "Why didn't you tell me that before?"

He walked over and studied the buyer before he spoke. Aguirre looked prosperous, an Anglo with a Mexican name, apparently; neatly dressed, and with a bartender's haircut. He wore a black suit and white tie, with a lodge emblem in his lapel. Fidel took the chair beside him.

"I'm Gary Fidel, Hogan's partner," he said.

The cattle buyer watched the wheel make its last few turns. "Glad to know you."

"Igualmente," said Fidel.

The little ball dropped, and the house man took all the money on the table. Aguirre glanced at Fidel briefly before studying the board. "What can I do for you?"

"You can make us another offer on those cattle

43

we're bringing up. John misunderstood my instructions. At sixteen dollars, we'll make less than a hundred on them. That's criminal."

Aguirre smiled. "Pity. I guess we'll have to break the law, then. It's in writing."

Why do I know this guy was lying? Fidel wondered. For one thing, Aguirre had the face and air of a friendly, talkative man; yet he was being very taciturn, and did not look at Fidel. And he knew as well as Fidel did that sixteen dollars a head in the railroad pens was ridiculous.

"How about sixteen fifty?" Fidel said, feeling demeaned. Why don't I get down on my knees? he thought dismally.

Aguirre smiled as he put a ten-dollar goldpiece at the junction of four numbers. "Are you saying you want half the money down? You don't think I'm good for it?"

Fidel got up. "No. I think you're good for it, Aguirre. Forget it. Send me something for Christmas. Out of what John's paying you."

Aguirre frowned and started to protest, but Fidel walked off.

John, he decided, is not only stupid, but a God-damn' thief.

He was absolutely determined, now, to get him out of the firm, and damn soon. And he'd better move that Gatling gun before many more nights. . . .

44

7

AT THE RAILWAY STATION, Fidel sent the wire to Mexico.
Hall was too busy to talk. At any rate, Fidel reckoned, he
had had his answer for the time being. He walked back
to International Street. A perspiring sentry in the little
hut on the American side nodded at him as he passed.

He had to wait a half-hour before the Mexican
freight agent returned from his siesta, dazed with
lunch and sleep. Fidel signed some papers securing
space on a flat-car, and returned to the office. It was
now past three o'clock. Waiting for the train-whistle,
he opened the big check book and studied the balance.
Four hundred and twenty-three dollars.

How much would it take to buy Hogan out?

Tipping back in the chair, he studied the blistered
plaster of the ceiling. If they split the blanket today,
Hogan would get a little over two hundred, plus what
they brought back from Mexico; about twenty-three
hundred for his share.

Pitiful.

Aside from the value of the gun—a dream at this
moment—Fidel was worth a little over two thousand
dollars, after a lifetime of hard work. Take care of
yourself, knuckle-head, he thought: All you've really
got is a little brain and a lot of brawn.

A train hooted hoarsely up the valley. With a sigh, he
locked the desk. As he walked out, he kicked Hogan's
roll of bedding in disgust.

But optimism began to tickle his ribs while he watched a diamond-stack locomotive, creaking and steaming, bang a half-dozen cars onto a siding. He thought of new business, of kissing Allie, of bringing back a bag of Mexican gold in return for Fort Hogan. Life might yet improve. A railroad man gave him the invoices on his shipment and he checked out the crates and barrels on the splintered dock. The heaviest items were flasks of mercury in wooden cases. There were some short lengths of iron rails to be used in making a grizzly at a gold mine near La Ventana. There were three barrels of provisions.

When he finished, he looked at his watch. Four o'clock. Where the hell was John? Four Mexican workmen were standing by to move his freight onto a Guaymas-bound car. *"Momentito,"* he told them, and gave them a dollar to go over and quench their thirst.

John, you whiskey-head, where are you now with our money? Back at the Palace Saloon? A feeling of foreboding climbed onto his back like an invalid needing a ride. He had seen Hogan put five hundred dollars in gold on a table and invite half the whores in Nogales to join him in a drink. . . .

Business was livelier now in the saloon. The cigar smoke was heavy as woodsmoke. Early closers were having a cold beer, early gamblers crowded the gaming tables. He heard Hogan's voice, shouting a laugh. In apprehension, he ran his eye along the bar, but did not see him. Then he heard a bray of laughter at the roulette table, looked quickly that way, and groaned. Oh, my God, he thought. The load on his back was now like a mule.

John sat near the wheel, a glass of beer and a shot-glass of rum at his elbow. In his nut-brown beard a little cigar like a mesquite twig puffed, as he stacked the gold coins he had just won.

"Don't fool with me, *cabrón!*" he shouted at the Mexican croupier. "I'll break your damned bank!"

"*Sí, señor,*" said the croupier, blank-faced. Walking over, Fidel scowled. No Mexican liked to be called *cabrón.*

He leaned down, picked up one of the neat stacks of gold coins, and counted. . . . Hogan turned on him and looked up into his face.

"Put 'em back, pardner!" he said. "I'll kill you if you break my run!"

Fidel's eyes polled the stacks of coins, bitterly. There were nine stacks and a few loose coins, each stack worth two hundred dollars. John had lost almost two thousand dollars of the firm's money. He heard him arguing and threatening, saw him throw down the rest of his rum as he studied Fidel's face. Fidel felt shocked, as though he had been hit with a rock. He was aware of men he knew watching him.

"Come over to the bar, John," he said. "Let's have a little tate-a-tay about finance. There's something about company funds you don't seem to understand."

Someone chuckled. The croupier held up on spinning the ball down the track as the wheel revolved.

"Get out of here!" Hogan jeered. "Haven't you got brains enough not to break up a run? I've just won back six hundred I'd lost! On one spin!"

"You're running the wrong way, John, and with my money. Come on."

Hogan said, "Oh, *hell!* You really have the gift, man." He glared around the table. "Anybody takes this chair, I will personally break their jaw." He got up.

"Put the money in the sack," Fidel said. He was surprised at how calm he sounded; as if he were driven into bankruptcy every day.

Hogan faked a punch at Fidel's jaw, but snatched up the canvas sack lying on the floor near his polished, pointed boot. He swept the clinking gold into it, but yanked the bag away when Fidel tried to take it from him. Hogan was almost weeping with rage. He had been on the point of winning back all he had lost.

In a pig's eye.

"I'll have a beer," Fidel told the bartender. "Make that a rum. Double," he added.

"Nothing for me," John Hogan declared, piously. "By the way," he said, with a show of belligerence, "I was at the office a while ago and found all my gear from Allie's there. What's going on?"

"You've been evicted for lewd and lascivious conduct. Listen to me, John. Can you hear me all right?"

"I hear you, parson."

"There's eighteen hundred dollars in that sack. The

company was worth forty-three hundred an hour ago, including four hundred we've got left in the bank. You've just lost two thousand. That leaves you five hundred dollars. Do you follow me?"

Hogan called to a bartender, his hand raised. "Rum shooter and a beer back," he said.

The bartender brought Fidel's double, and he drank half of it quickly.

"I follow you," Hogan said.

"I make your goodbye money at five hundred and twenty-five," Fidel said. "I'll keep what's in the bank. We're quits."

"And what about the, uh, assets?" argued Hogan, furiously. He waited, his eyes half-shut, puffing on the cigar.

"You get half of Fort Hogan when and if I manage to sell it." He rummaged in the money-bag and counted out five hundred and twenty dollars in double eagles. He put a half-eagle from his pocket with the money on the bar.

"I've got more coming than that!" Hogan said.

"And you'll get it, if you aren't careful," Fidel warned. He felt little jumps of energy in his muscles; carbonation popping in his head. He had never been closer to killing a man. "Don't overlook the fact that you've just embezzled half the company's assets. I don't know whether I can pull myself out of this hole or not. If I can't, I'll probably kill you."

"You try, hombre."

"We'll see John Scrivner tomorrow morning and get

49

the papers drawn up." He was almost gasping with rage.

"Better sleep on it," Hogan said. His drinks came, and he put the rum back and took a swallow of beer. "Don't do anything you'll regret."

"The only thing I regret doing, you just squared for me. Going into partnership with you."

"Take my advice," Hogan said with contempt. "Get yourself a wagon and buy people's old clothes. That's the only way a natural fool like you will ever make a living. You don't know a—"

Fidel turned back and looked at him. Hogan puffed on the cigar, grinning. "I've still got a few things up at the whorehouse," he said. "I'll be up later and get them."

"Suit yourself." Fidel started to turn away, but frowned. "I don't follow. What whorehouse?"

"Phoebe! Robin! Oriole!" Hogan sneered. "The women she writes to. Don't be so God-damned thick-headed. I mean Allie's whorehouse. It only takes one whore to—"

Hogan's cigar was driven back into his beard as Fidel's fist landed. A man yelled in delight. The bartender, who had just brought Hogan's drinks, tried to get an arm between them.

"Boys! Now, wait a minute—look here—"

Fidel fired another punch at Hogan's head, but the big man ducked away. Then Hogan brought a round-house swing from way back, and Fidel lifted his arm to block it, and caught it on the ribs. He did not feel

50

pain, but it knocked the wind out of him. The rage in him was like a glee, a baffled anger he had carried so long it had begun to feel like a chronic pain; but now it was free and going wild. He was shouting things at Hogan that he only half understood as he went at him.

He was being hit, and he was hitting. Hogan was enjoying it, too. His mouth was bleeding, but he was grinning. His right eyebrow was skinned and bloody. They circled each other like wild dogs, the men around them shouting. Chet Hardin was there, backing his boss. Fidel saw that John had buckled on his Colt when he picked up his gear at the office, but so far, at least, it had not occurred to him to try to draw it.

Suddenly Fidel was down on the floor, his head swimming. Men were shouting. He saw Hogan standing back, pale, bloody and gasping, too winded to taunt him. Fidel's head cleared as though a wind had blown through it. He gave himself a moment to catch his breath, then staggered up and went toward Hogan in a crouch. He saw, to his surprise, that John was seemingly in worse shape than he was, his chest heaving, his arms held low; knowing him, he knew exactly what was going to happen.

Hogan was going to try to finish him off while he could—with a flourish.

Johnny came at him with a long right-hand swing, which Fidel ducked; then a left, then another right, accompanied by a grunt of total effort. Fidel kept backing, letting his arms hang to rest his shoulders.

"Hit me, you bastard!" he taunted. "Come on, stupid."

John kept coming, grunting with each swing, and the moment he stopped coming, Fidel was on him, a jab, a right hand to the head, another jab. The first time he felt pain he felt it in his right hand, when a blow to the jaw landed. He was coming to his senses; he could feel pain, now; savage anger had burned down like a fuse.

Hogan staggered against a table. He put his hand out to steady himself, and Fidel chunked in another right, this time to the chin. He knew from the sweet feel of it that it had gone to the point of Hogan's jaw with all the power he had left. Dropping to all fours, Johnny Hogan tried to get up again, but sprawled flat.

Fidel looked around. The room had bent slightly out of focus, and he was gasping for breath. A man offered him a blue bandana. He wiped his nose and mouth and looked at the handkerchief. He was bleeding, all right; like a stuck pig.

"What did he say?" the man asked him, eagerly. "What was it all about?"

Fidel hoped no one had heard, but knew some of them must have. "Oh, just—money matters," he panted. "Somebody give his gun to the marshal, huh? Till he gets straightened out—"

"I'll walk with you," another man said. "You going back to your room?"

It was Tom Hall. When had he arrived? "Yeah. Okay. Listen," Fidel said. "Need to talk to you."

"All right. Here—drink this—"

Hall handed him someone's shot-glass of whiskey.

He drank it, and they left. On the sidewalk, the telegrapher said:

"You're going to have a few aches and pains, Gary. I'll walk up to Doctor Mix's with you. He'll give you some powders or whatnot."

Fidel tested to see whether his nose was still bleeding. In his mind, worries were swarming like fire ants. He snuffled. His nose was completely stopped up, but did not seem to be bleeding. He spat some blood in the street. His mouth tasted like old pennies.

"No, listen," he said. "I'm not that bad off. But I'll tell you what—you might pick up something at the drug store and bring it to my room."

"All right. Go to the hotel and wash up. I've got my father's pharmaceutical bag in my hotel room. I'll bring it over. I'm moving to Allie's tonight and I'll be carrying some things up anyway."

8

ON THE WAY UPSTAIRS, Fidel bought a quart of whiskey in the hotel bar. He saw men eyeing him, and two or three spoke. He grinned. He knew he must look like the survivor of an Apache ambush. His head throbbed and his jaw ached. He hoped he was not going to lose a tooth. The key rattled as he unlocked his door.

He poured an inch of whiskey into an alkali-stained glass, then flopped on the bed with one arm bent under his head, exhausted. When he closed his eyes, his head spun. He squinted at the alarm clock on the marble-topped dresser: a quarter to six. He smelled the charcoal smoke of Mexican supper fires.

There was a kind of scratching on the door.

"*Mánde?*" he called.

"*El baño, señor.*"

He hoisted himself from the bed and got a dime from the dresser. He tipped the Mexican maid who had filled the tub. Then he stripped off his double-breasted shirt—torn beyond repair—and pulled clean underclothing, socks and a shirt from a drawer. Everything was neatly laid out, Army style, very fussily. He had been a bachelor too long; he was becoming compulsively neat.

As he slid into the water with a luxurious groan, he remembered that four hundred and twenty-three dollars was waiting in the bank for Hogan to withdraw! He gave up the soak he needed, washed quickly and rasped his skin—with a towel stiff from the clothesline. Then he dressed and hurried back to his room over the street.

. . . And not only the bank account to change, he remembered, but the office lock! And probably a dozen other tag-ends of his business with Hogan. He had about two hours of daylight left, and the train to Sonora left at nine-thirty the next morning.

And out there in the hills a Gatling gun was waiting to be stolen.

And what was he going to do about Allie?

What *could* he do? The men who had heard the words would tell other men, and they would all tell their wives. The word "whore" would be whispered. And some would believe it, for people craved scandal as they did candy. He sat on the end of the bed and scowled out the window.

How much did he believe himself? The bird-names—the long sleeves—the lack of family: all the little mysteries which had somehow endeared her to him. They could be bad news, now.

He reached for the bottle of Mountain Brook and had another drink. It didn't matter what she'd been, he thought piously. The hell it didn't!

And what was that charade about John having loose women in his room? Hypocrisy! if she herself had come from a sporting house.

The code said that there were two kinds of women, but he had never really believed that, even though he had not met any whores he would have cared particularly to marry. But he could understand how circumstances might force a young girl into prostitution. And yet . . . He took another angry drink, picturing her on a bed, naked, with a half-drunken man with his trousers off. She was urging him to get on with it . . . there was another man waiting. . . .

"God damn it!" he said, loudly.

A knock on the door. "Come in," he said. It was Hall, carrying a small black leather case.

He had left his coat somewhere, and looked almost human in a shirt without a tie. "I thought I heard you talking to somebody," he said.

"Myself. Plenty to discuss."

55

Hall sat on the bed and opened the bag.

"As far as I can tell," he said, "most of these drugs are for constipation. How are your bowels?"

Fidel laughed. "Anything for toothache?"

Hall fingered the little tubes of pills in racks.

"Peacock's Bromide. . . . No, that would make you sleepy. Hmm. Here's one—phenacetin with opium. That ought to do it. Wash it down with a little whiskey."

"How about some whiskey for yourself?"

"I don't mind." Hall found another tumbler and poured himself a drink.

"What did you hear about the fight?"

"I was in the street when somebody stuck his head out the door and yelled."

"So you don't know what it was about?"

"No."

"It was over money. If anybody asks you, tell them that. Hogan gambled away half our assets. I paid him off for what he had coming out of the company, and he thought he should have more."

Hall laughed. "So you gave it to him."

"So I gave it to him. Right now I've got two problems. Make that three. Number one, I've got to open a new account before he can withdraw what's left. Number two, I should be in Sonora tomorrow. Number three, I've got to move that damned Gatling gun."

Hall held the whiskey up to the light. "I'll walk up to the bank with you. Can't Sonora wait?"

"No, sir. I've got a date near Rincon. The party might lose faith in me if I don't show. These people will not hang around long. They're like coyotes, smart and restless. For them, a day is like a month."

"True. First things first: The bank is closed, but I saw Leo Lucas inside as I went past just now. You'd better get up there. I'll get Dad's buggy and haul my stuff up to Allie's. And here's your gun. I fixed it during my lunch hour. It's loaded, so be careful. Can you carry this pharmaceutical bag up to Allie's?"

Fidel explained to Leo Lucas, the bank president, that he and John Hogan had decided to dissolve the company. He signed papers for a new account, with an opening balance of what he had left from Hogan's gambling spree, and the leavings in their account.

A warm, dusty wind, rich with woodsmoke, blew from the east as he walked up the hill. He had had a faint hope that the cabinet would not be in session on the boarding house porch, but even Miss Peacock was there to watch him open the gate. Their eyes shone with inquisitiveness as he approached. They looked at the gun on his hip and the scrapes and swellings on his face, but no one asked what had happened.

"I'll tell you all about it one day," he muttered. "It's gettin' to be a tough town."

"Mercy!" he heard Miss Peacock whisper to Arthur, as he went into the house. He could hear Allie in the kitchen, and looked in. Small and industrious, she stood at the sink, apparently trying to polish a carrot with a scouring pad. Some outlandish idea of Barenar's?

"Is Hall's room unlocked?" he asked. "I've got a case of his."

She looked around. "Yes, just put it—" Then she peered at him, and gasped: "You've been in a fight! Oh, Gary, how could you?"

Fidel shrugged. "There's a right time for everything."

Allie laid the supper things in the stone sink and came to him. She stood on tiptoe and sniffed. "You've been drinking, too. Your *breath!* Beer and whiskey, by the smell of you."

Who are you to lecture me? he thought. He tried to close a door in his mind, through which he saw her naked on a rumpled bed.

"I had a couple to celebrate splitting the blanket with Hogan."

"Oh, I hope—! Was it because I put him out?"

"That was part of it. The other part was that he gambled away half our money."

He turned to walk down the hall, but she caught his arm. "I didn't mean to scold, Gary—I do understand. You aren't angry, are you?"

"No."

"I know that men—do things impulsively sometimes. . . ."

He waited, studying her face, the anxious blue eyes behind schoolmarmish glasses she wore sometimes, the impish features.

58

"But I just couldn't have him bringing women to the house. Miss Peacock said something once, indirectly—her position as a teacher, or something. I had to have him out."

"All right!" Fidel said, impatiently. "He knows now. Forget it."

She looked surprised and hurt. "But I shouldn't have asked you to do my dirty work for me. I suppose I'm afraid of the man. There's violence in him."

"There's less tonight than there was this morning, I think," Fidel said. "Although I wouldn't count on it. Let me see something—"

He set the case down and reached up to remove her spectacles. He wiped a tiny droplet of water from one lens. She waited, puzzled. He squinted through the lenses, pursed his lips, and put them back on her nose, carefully.

"I wear reading glasses when I'm doing the books," he said. "Must have more prism in mine than you have. These seem perfectly clear."

He saw that he had defused her, actually frightened her. She adjusted the glasses. "—I only use them when the light is poor, before I turn on the lights. . . ."

Fidel went on to Hall's room. Whatever Allie wore them for, it was not for better vision, because there was no correction at all to the lenses.

9

WHILE THE OTHERS ATE, Fidel helped Tom Hall carry in a trunk and some other articles. The last item in the back of Doctor Hall's Stanhope buggy was a blanket. Hall peeled it back to reveal two rifles and some hand-guns.

"I'll carry in the hand-guns," he said, "but I'd better explain about the rifles. . . ."

"What's up?" Fidel asked, with a grimace. "Is Hogan looking for me?"

"No. But when I went to the livery barn to get my buggy, Chet Hardin was there ordering three saddle horses for eight o'clock. One of them was that mare you like. Hardin and Ruben Lara are the two men Hogan usually takes along when he buys cattle, aren't they?"

"God damn," Fidel said softly, nodding.

"So I told Harney to saddle up my father's appaloosa and another riding horse, for seven-thirty. That's about now. I think you ought to leave first, and I'll follow ten minutes later. In case anybody decides to follow you."

"I don't get this," Fidel said. "Haven't you had enough action since you quit the Army?"

"Noise and action are two different things. Two Spanish Mausers can lay down enough noise to scare off any three men. Then we can move your Gatling gun. I don't know where you've got it hidden, but if we can take up positions anywhere near it—"

Picking up one of the bolt-action rifles, Fidel said: "It would be perfect. Where'd you get Spanish Mausers?"

"A Mexican sold them to me. Stolen from the Mexican army. They hold twelve shots, and they're so much better than anything we have that it's criminal."

"Now I know everything but why you're doing it," Fidel said.

"To keep you out of trouble. If you go out there alone, you're liable to kill somebody, or get killed. The way I understand it, if you lose the gun, you'll go under?"

"I may anyway. Are you buying in with me? You wouldn't have to worry about being partners with Hogan any more."

"No. I've still got an offer in for Bob Eldred's gunshop. This is strictly recreation."

"I'll try to make it worth your while," Fidel smiled.

Fidel jogged as far as the wide, sandy river-bottom, and pulled up among the mesquites on the sandbars to wait. There was a cold, wet smell of mud and brush. The low hills stood out faintly against the rusty night, a last green tint flowing over them. The pockets of his denim coat were heavy with long-nosed 7-millimeter shells Hall had given him. He dismounted by an uprooted tree on the sandbar and tied the horse to a snag. The gun loaded easily, twelve shots more or less dumped into the magazine. He worked the bolt once to get the feel of it; the follower was smooth and almost silent as the cartridge went into the chamber. He extracted and caught the shell, replaced it in the gun, and put it on safety.

He heard a horse on the road, and felt a ripple of gooseflesh. He thought he would be able to make out the form of the rider. He and Hall had agreed on a signal: an owl-hoot. But if it were not Hall, the horseman would still not necessarily be Hogan or one of his men.

The horse was in a purposeful jog, unhurried but not lazy. It came from the shadows a hundred feet away, the rider straight up in the saddle. It was too dark to see whether he was carrying a rifle. When he was thirty feet away, Fidel made the owl-hoot. The man pulled the horse in and returned the call.

Fidel joined him.

"Anything new in town?" he asked.

"Not that I noticed."

"About a mile from here we'll ride up the hill to a ridge. It overlooks the canyon. How fast can this gun be fired?"

"As fast as you can work the bolt; and the kick is like a love-pat. Winchester seems to think a gun has to kill the soldier as well as the enemy."

The horses scuffed along the sandy ruts, and darkness blew in like coal smoke, obliterating the desert hills. He began to watch for the skewed telephone pole. Suddenly they both heard something on the road behind them, and twisted to look back. Several horses could be heard coming at a trot.

He swerved his horse through the brush up a rocky hillside. It was fortunate that the animal could see better than he could, because the night was full now, moonless and hot. They rode uphill for a half-minute before reining in. They could still hear the trotting horses when they halted.

"That's them," he muttered. "John always works the tail off a rent horse."

He led the way through the rocks toward the ridge which he knew was there somewhere in the sky. It was urgent to get out of earshot as fast as possible. It would be disastrous if the horses got to calling to each other. And also they had to be in position before Hogan's men reached the mine tunnel.

The riders clattering along below them suddenly reined in. Fidel halted his horse, sharply, and Hall came up beside him. They listened. There were voices, and the snorting of winded horses. Then a match flared, surprisingly bright in the darkness; then another and another, orange explosions in the night, that died as they lighted their smokes. In a short time the wind, sweeping up the hillside, brought the aroma of cigars. John would not last long in Indian country, Fidel reflected.

Hogan's men rested their horses for about five minutes before starting the climb up the canyon to the mine. Fidel was heading for the ridge above it. At last they heard hoofs scuffing up the mine road, and they let their mounts start to climb again.

10

THEY LEFT THE HORSES below the ridge and began
climbing afoot. Carrying the Mausers, they picked
their way carefully through the shattered boulders and
tough little trees that hissed like cats in the hot wind.
Fidel could see the ground clearly, though the sky was
like blued steel; its vault was frosted with icy splinters
of stars and galaxies, and glaring swaths like incan-
descent gas. There was starshine if not moonlight,
light enough for an owl-eyed gunman like Ruben Lara
to be a menace. With chalked sights, he could put a
bullet in the five-ring in the dark, Hogan claimed.
Damn him, Fidel thought, we'll have to scare the
bowels out of them all before they have a chance to
collect their wits.

On a bald path that marked the divide, the hill fell
abruptly into the canyon. Fidel touched Hall's arm,
and they knelt to wait. It was not long before they
heard, a hundred feet below them and far to the right,
the ring of hoofs. It was a carefree clatter that heart-
ened Fidel a little, for surprise was their big weapon.
He heard the sounds of the horses being halted at the
mine, then of the men dismounting, and of John's big
Mexican-silver spurs clinking.

They tried to make them out, but the darkness hid
what was going on. He tried to decode Hogan's plan: To
carry the crate back to town and hide it? No; too heavy;
too much work for a loafer like him. Bury it, then, or

hide it in another tunnel? Maybe. Or maybe in the brush. Nor would he put it past John simply to dump it somewhere out of spite, dead loss to everybody.

Then he heard an unmistakable sound, one that made him chuckle with relief, and made Hall grin. The squeak of a cork coming out of a whiskey bottle! It was John, all right! So the big man thought he was alone out here.

Okay, he thought, now what?

To lay down a sudden fire would stampede the horses and leave the men afoot. Did he want that? Not necessarily: they'd be all night getting back to town, might lay for them beside the road.

The alternative, to leave them mounted, had the disadvantage of enabling them to ride around all night trying to cut their sign.

He decided it would be best to scatter their horses—demoralize them, leave them blundering back down to the road thinking they were lucky to get out alive. He and Hall would avoid the road in returning to town. Fidel cupped his hand and whispered:

"I'll hike up the ridge to that little tree. Let me empty my gun, then open up while I'm reloading. Maybe we'd better move off a little ways before the second round so they won't home in on us."

"Fire well above them," Hall cautioned. "Don't kill anybody, or we'll wind up in court."

Fidel had crawled to a point about fifty feet above Hall when the enormous, booming crash of a gun reverberated through the hills. He hit the ground.

What the hell? Had Hall accidentally jumped the gun? Then a bullet hit near him, and he saw a spurt of flame in the canyon, and a second shot roared as another slug screamed off a rock near where he lay.

Jesus Christ! We're outlined against the stars! he realized. Lara had seen them.

Another gun roared, and then the third, the bullets slamming and ricocheting around him. Fidel rolled behind a shrub and jammed the Mauser against his shoulder. But it wouldn't fire. He swore and thumbed the gun off safety, picked a target of pale rock above the road, and fired. The gun-barrel lifted slightly, but the kick was surprisingly light. He heard the slug strike and go wailing off down the canyon.

He rocked the bolt and fired a second shot, then a third. He could feel the barrel heating up. He heard the men shouting. A couple of wild shots came back. He kept firing the Mauser until it went empty, and by that time there was a respectful silence below. The crashing firepower had intimidated Hogan's crowd, at least for the moment. As Hall began firing, Fidel, crawling away, could hear men yelling at each other, then a bottle smashing on a rock. The horses began running down the canyon, and a man bawled:

"Ho! Ho, Goddammit!"

Fidel reloaded, and as soon as Hall's gun went silent he began firing again. The men below were blundering around shouting at each other. Before long, he heard them retreating down the canyon. He reloaded and waited. But there was no more return fire.

They waited a half-hour. Then they got the horses and rode on up the ridge to a point where they could take a trail down into the canyon. They rode up to the mine road and started south. Fidel remembered the landmarks, now, mine ruins and heaps of rusting machinery. When they reached the mine, he dismounted and listened for a while, then beckoned to Hall to dismount. The telegrapher unlashed an Army entrenching tool from behind his saddle.

Everything was quiet. The long day, with its demands, had stolen his energy, and the work was not over yet. But he pumped himself up like a bellows to keep going. While Hall guarded the horses, he walked to the mine adit and lighted the lamp. He hurried down the tunnel to the drift where he had left the gun.

He found the crate and dragged it back to the main tunnel. At the end of it was a stope where the miners had blasted and dug before finally giving up and turning right. He moved enough rocks that he could bury the crate securely.

He stood up, massaging his back. John, I hope you're just a little dumber than I am, he thought. This is the last place you'd think of looking for it, if I know you. If I don't, it will be gone when I get back from Mexico.

When he went back, Hall retied the shovel, and they mounted. Fidel sniffed. "Doesn't that whiskey smell good? Maybe I can lick a little off the road. I've done harder things to make a dollar."

Hall laughed, but did not fulfill Fidel's hope by saying something like, Well, your troubles are over, Fidel—I'm buying in with you.

Nothing, of course, was ever that easy.

11

IT WAS ALREADY STIFLING in his room when he awoke the next morning. He sat up, dazed and alarmed. What was wrong? He knew instinctively that something was out of kilter somewhere. The train, of course! He had to be on it at ten o'clock. The nickel-plated alarm clock on the dresser said eight-thirty. He rolled out, groaning.

With some pain he washed his face. There was no time to shave. His eyebrow was swollen, his lip was puffed out. His mustache needed trimming, but where he was going no one would care. As he was pulling on a shirt, someone knocked.

"Mánde?" Fidel called.

"Una señora desea conferencia—el instrumento!" a boy's voice said.

What instrumento?

Oh, yes, the Montezuma's famous telephone. There were over two hundred of them on the system. He tipped the boy. Hall might be calling from the railroad station. Or even Allie, who had kept Doctor Hall's telephone. He went downstairs, stuffing in his shirttail. At the end of the registration desk a big oaken instrument was bolted to the wall. The desk clerk offered him the black cone called a receiver.

He spoke forcibly: "Hello! This is Gary Fidel. Hello?"

A woman's voice came faintly, high-pitched and thin, through the muted sounds of the wire. "Gary?"

"Yes! This is Gary Fidel!" he shouted.

"Are you still going to La Ventana today?" Allie asked.

"Yes!"

"What?" she asked faintly.

"*Yes!*" he bawled. "I'll—"

"You haven't forgotten?"

"No! I'll be right up! Fry an egg for me."

"Try and what?" Allie asked.

"Never mind!" he roared. "I'll come up."

If they'd open the back window, he thought, she'd be able to hear him. It was only three blocks. He sprinted upstairs, finished dressing, buckled on his Colt, and locked the door.

He smelled bacon frying as he entered. The place seemed empty. Mr. Cleaveland would be out taking his long constitutional, Mr. Montana was at his drugstore, and there was no telling what Miss Peacock was up to. But Allie—all in black, dammit!—entered the dining room as he came in the other door: black shirtwaist, floor-sweeping skirts, long sleeves, a veritable crow of a little woman. She smiled timidly. The clear glasses dangled on her breast by a fine gold chain.

"I decided it was something about frying eggs,"

she said. "So I'm frying some bacon and eggs."

"Fine, fine. I've only got a few minutes."

"It will be just a minute, I won't slow you down. But there are some papers I wanted to give you—sit down, Gary, I'll bring you some melon. Bernard always like to start with fruit."

"If Saint Bernard liked melon," Fidel said soberly, "that's good enough for me."

She regarded him uncertainly, did not smile until he finally grinned. She hurried into the kitchen. Fidel sat where a single place was laid, and saw some documents before it. He picked one up. It was written in French, apparently, an "*Acte de Naissance*," dated 1846, in Marseilles. The other was also in French, at least in a similar foreign language, a "*Diplome de l'Ecole des Arts et Métiers*." Bernard, evidently, had become an engineer in Paris in 1870. Or something.

Congratulation, Bernard. What does that have to do with me?

Allie brought a plate of fried eggs, bacon, and toast. "It's hot—be careful." As he started eating, she put on her spectacles and studied the papers.

"You might need these to find what I want," she said. "I hope I'm not asking too much. . . . I'd like to get his gold *milagro*—the heart—first. And then, if you could ask whether he left any personal effects—he had a nice watch, a little knife, some things like that. If you could get them for me? And ask whether he left any debts, or even money in a bank. Or perhaps a last message for me."

70

"I can try," Fidel mumbled.

"You might need his birth certificate or diploma, and my marriage license."

Fidel glanced at the marriage certificate. "San Francisco, eh? State of California. I've been there. Small world."

Allie ignored his whimsy. He read on. "Witnesses—hmm, Phoebe McCartney, Robin Coe. Bird ladies, eh? And Father John J. O'Toole. Five years ago?"

"Mm—hm. Of course, he's been dead for a year," Allie said. "And I actually never seen—saw much of him. He didn't want me living in mining towns, so I'd live somewhere not too far off, like—like this. When I think back, we were almost like strangers. . . ."

"What was your maiden name, Allie?" When he said maiden, he faltered, and saw Allie look down. Of course most modest women would, at such a word.

"Fitzgerald," she said. "My father was a railroad worker. My mother died when I was six. I had three sisters, but one died."

"Could have been worse," Fidel grinned. "Most railroad workers in California were Chinese when you were born. Your name might have been Chow. Allie Chow."

She smiled, doubtfully.

He stuffed the last of the food in his mouth and stood up. "Fine, I'll talk to the *padre* and the *alcade*. See what I scratch up."

"Just a minute. You might have a better chance if your mustache wasn't so—weren't so ragged. Stand still."

71

She took a small pair of sewing scissors from an Indian bowl on the sideboard, and began, her lips pursed, to clip off some of the hairs beginning to curl down into his mouth. She finished and looked into his eyes. Her expression seemed to plead and accuse. He felt guilty and excited.

"That's better," she said softly. "You will be careful?"

"Oh sure. I'll travel by first class mule. Avoid strangers and cardsharps. Drink only blackberry brandy."

He was thinking of something else amusing to say when she kissed him. It was as electrical an experience as the first time he tried to change a light bulb at the hotel. His nerves twanged. Her lips were not drawn up like a prune, but soft, velvety, and clinging. And he smelled a perfume, almost like vanilla or marshmallow; maybe it was vanilla, but more than likely it was some French concoction of Bare-nar's. It hurt his swollen lip, but took his breath. He put his hands on her upper arms, but she pulled away, removed her glasses, and said,

"Thank you, Gary! God speed."

He gathered up the papers. "I'd better leave your marriage license," he said. "Too important, and I won't need it."

72

12

AT THE RAILROAD STATION, the mixed train was already in position when he arrived. He had dressed in the clothes he always wore to Mexico, a khaki shirt, denim work pants, boots, and a straw sombrero. With the heavy bandoliers crossed over his chest, and his mustache, he looked like a revolutionary. In addition to his Army revolver, he carried one of Hall's Mausers in a saddle boot, and was lugging his saddle.

He had left orders for the lock on his office to be changed immediately. He had bought several boxes of forty-five caliber ammunition and filled his bandoliers, and stuffed a dozen sticks of dynamite into his bedroll. He had withdrawn a hundred dollars in gold. He might have expenses; might even have to buy back that golden heart of Bernard's.

He walked into the telegraph office. Hall was on duty, wearing a green eyeshade.

"Pretty quiet here, for a man of action," Fidel told him. "Ought to get into the export-import trade."

"Speaking of import," Hall said, "there's a cattle buyer named Aguirre waiting for you. He's on the bench outside."

"That's Hogan's problem," Fidel said. "My problem is bailing out that mining machinery on the siding. Now, if you were to buy in with me. . . ."

Hall looked pained. "I'd like to, but. . . . I'm waiting on Eldred, you know. Why don't we talk about it after this, er, gun thing is settled?"

"It can't be settled until I take a shipment of freight down—some way of disguising what I'm carrying. And I can't take the freight down until I pay for it."

"Then what are you going for?"

". . . Some errands I need to run for myself and Allie." He heard the train give two bleats. "Thanks for the help last night, Tom. Wasn't that exciting?"

Hall smiled. The telegraph key began to rattle, and he turned to grab a pencil.

Aguirre, the cattle buyer, looked at Fidel and twisted one end of his mustaches. He came to where Fidel was walking toward a passenger car, carrying blanket roll, saddle and Mauser.

"Got a minute?" he asked.

"No," Fidel said. He knew what was coming, and felt like surprising the man by hitting him in the mouth before he could start talking.

"I heard at the hotel that you've bought out John Hogan."

"You'll hear frogs have wings, if you hang around the Montezuma long enough. *Adiós.*"

"Wait a minute," Aguirre said. "We have a business deal. You owe me one hundred head of cattle in thirty days."

"No, my friend, that's Hogan's deal. Talk to him about it. Throw the fear into him. It was his share of the assets when we split up—the killing we were making off you."

Aguirre said sternly: "I don't know where you got

74

the idea you can buy out a partner and write off your obligations. The sale is a binding obligation of Great Western Trading Company."

"Bullshit," laughed Fidel. "I've just reorganized. This very minute."

"I'll expect the cattle in thirty days. Otherwise I'll have to take you to court."

Fidel patted his shoulder, laughing. "Oh, you're tough, Aguirre. And I'll explain about the kind of deals you make behind a man's back! Other cattle buyers around town might be interested to hear about it, not to mention the City Attorney."

He climbed the steps of a dusty Arizona and New Mexico car and went inside, looking for a seat. Of course, he thought furiously, he's right. I do owe him the damned cattle. At the far end of the car, two men sat looking at him; another man in the facing seat turned to stare. Johnny Hogan, his straw sombrero on the back of his head, was smiling and nodding at him.

"Sit down. Make yourself at home," Hogan said to him.

"Where do you think you're going?" Fidel asked. He sat on the arm of the seat across the aisle from the men. They were all dressed like working cowboys—spurs on their boots, chaps, work clothes, saddles dumped in the space between the seats.

"I'm still in the cattle trade," Johnny Hogan said. "I had my goodbye money, and I was able to raise a little. I'll start slow and build up. Got an order from your friend Aguirre just now."

Fidel noticed that his gold bracelet and rings were missing. "You already had an order," he said. "I just told Aguirre to talk to you about it."

"No, no, Fidel—that's part of the company obligations. Separate deal entirely." Hogan grinned, but not very widely. There was a black scab on his lower lip. His right eye was dark and swollen, and there was a patch of skin off his forehead.

Fidel looked at Ruben Lara, Hogan's part-time cowboy. He was built like a bull, a huge-shouldered fighting bull, massive, thick-necked, and dark. He was dark-skinned and humorless. His famous owl's-eyes were black slits below a ledge of bone.

"You're going to get shot one of these days, Lara," Fidel said pleasantly. "Opening up on a man that way. You might get drilled with a Spanish Mauser like this one."

"I don't know what you're talking about," Lara muttered.

"All I can say," Hogan came in, "is that if there was some gunplay last night, Ruben wasn't in on it, or somebody would be dead today. Man," he laughed, "you take things so *hard!* I had a little gambling spree yesterday, and I got beat up for something stupid I said. By the way, I'm sorry about that. Tell the little lady John said excuse me. But I had some fun, I'm back in business, and all you've got is a long face. So who's being foolish?"

"Fine, John. If it meant that much to you, okay. I'm a long-faced sort, I admit—but a shenanigan like last

76

night's wouldn't be worth six thousand dollars to me. Still, I guess it's really a matter of how you look at things."

Fidel started back down the car to another seat, but Hogan stood up.

"Hey," he said. "It was two thousand, not six."

"The asset," Fidel said. "Fort Hogan. You forfeited your right to it last night when you tried to steal it. You went so far as to try to kill me. That told me I had nothing to lose by stealing it myself. Which I did."

He sat down on a woven wickerwork seat, wriggled into a comfortable slouch with his hat tipped down over his face, but made sure he could see his ex-partner through his eyelashes.

13

IN MIDAFTERNOON, ON A hot and windy plain, Hogan and his cowhands got up and carried their gear forward. Fidel collected his and walked to the rear platform. Dust clouds scurried along as the train slowed. It was now past three o'clock, but the heat was even more insistent than it had been at noon, a dry, remorseless heat that had fired the great Sonoran Desert and the mountains a few miles east as hard as pottery. From the tawny soil grew paloverde, mesquite, and a few hardy grasses. Fidel gazed toward the bluish ridge of hills a couple of miles east. In the wiry desert vegetation lay a few buildings, and corrals of stone and cactus. A herd of cattle were penned in a corral not far from the railroad tracks.

As the train slowed, a few small adobe structures moved past, then a gray mountain of mesquite, a wooden water tank, a small station building without a platform, and some loading chutes. He saw Hogan drop from the moving car and trot a few steps before heading toward a couple of men standing near the station. Some children gazed at the locomotive, squealing in excitement. Fidel waited until the train stopped, to dismount with his saddle, rifle, blanket roll and little sack of food.

Hogan was talking to one of the men before the station, a tall man with fine black mustaches. He wore leather *pantalones,* a collarless shirt, and a tall straw sombrero. His name was Gardea, the rancher from whom they had bought most of their cattle. The other man was the one-eyed telegrapher who passed Fidel's messages to the Yaquis. Fidel left his belongings near the train.

". . . Thirty-five head," Hogan was saying in English as he approached. *"Comprende?"* Chet Hardin and Ruben Lara were coming toward the station but staying at a respectful distance, to let Hogan handle matters.

"That's less than we ordered, but we've had some problems, see? *Comprende?* You understand? But I've got five hundred dollars, *oro,* right here. . . ."

The rancher looked at Fidel. He spoke in Spanish. *"Qué dice?"* he asked.

So Fidel had to explain it. Hogan could not be both-

78

ered to learn a primitive language like Spanish. He said they had dissolved the company, that he was too short of funds to buy any cattle this trip, but hoped to be buying again soon. He regretted having put Señor Gardea to so much trouble. He would not even be needing the wagon and mules he had ordered, but would pay for any expense he had put the rancher to, and would like to rent the big bay horse he had used before.

"Señor Hogan wishes to buy thirty-five head of steers, I understand," he finished.

"Did it take all that palaver to say I want thirty-five cattle?" Hogan muttered.

Gardea was a gentleman. He forgave them their sins, and called to one of the boys to run to the horse corral. Tell the men to bring—how many horses? he asked Fidel, looking at Hogan's men. Five horses.

Fidel thanked him and paid in advance for three days' use of the horse. "I may be back sooner," he said.

There was no cafe in the little station, but the *patrón* told the telegrapher, Gregorio, to bring a bottle of tequila, two limes, and some glasses. They sat on a bench at the north side of the building, where there was shade, and he poured three glasses of clear liquor. He sliced the limes and each man chewed on a half, and then drank some of the fierce liquor. It went down like fishhooks and started a fire in the gullet, but it was good for the disposition. After a couple of drinks Fidel could almost look into Hogan's jeering face without clenching his fists.

79

Presently he set the glass down. The boy had returned with his horse, and the others were being ridden over. "I thank you, my friend. I'd better get started."

"You'll stay at Ojo de Agua tonight?" asked the rancher.

"Quién sabe?" Fidel said. John could not understand the question, probably, but it was better to be vague.

His horse had been saddled, the rifle-boot installed properly, blanket roll tied behind the saddle, and the boy stood nearby for a tip. The telegrapher came to hand up the small sack of food.

"Qué son las noticias?" asked Fidel.

"Buenas," said the telegrapher. He had one keen black eye, and another like a discolored ball of salt.

. . . Now Fidel knew that word had been passed to the Yaqui runner in the region that he was coming. He sorted the reins in his fingers, waved goodbye, and jogged toward the hills. The blue was already deepening on the mountains, shadows had begun to stripe the hillsides like tigers. With luck, he would make the mining hamlet of La Barranca before dark.

14

THE SUN ON HIS back was like a branding iron, but within an hour he was in the hills. There was shade, and the sun was sinking. The wagon road shovelled into the red hillside was steep and rough, easy enough for the horse, but brutal when he drove a wagon. The horse was strong, spooky like most Mexican horses; he had to watch it, or he would suddenly be on a walking trip of the Sierra Tipic. A scrap of paper would send it into hysterics.

He halted a couple of times to rest the horse and study his backtrail. It was possible that Hogan had come down to buy cattle; in fact, he thought that was what he had done, because he needed money. But it was also possible that he was thinking of the eight thousand dollars the Yaquis were going to pay for the Gatling gun. That worried Fidel now! Doing all the work, and being shot for the profits later. Knowing how Hogan's head worked, he did not think he would report him to the Mexican Army. At best, that would bring him a few hundred pesos. Hogan would go for the whole kitty. I should have killed him the other night, he thought bitterly. Buried him in a mine-shaft. No one would ever miss him enough to start excavating.

Rounding a hill in the dusk, he heard goat bells, sounds of children and dogs, a rooster crowing. The village of La Barranca was just ahead. He would stay with a marooned German family named Fröck, and pick up his "mail." A Yaqui would bring it sometime after dark . . . a few words of mixed Spanish and Cáhita.

He smelled supper fires and beans cooking, and his mouth watered. He was following a wide barranca now, groves of leafless trees like gnarled apple trees

81

on its hillsides. There were mines in the hills, all of them long-since deserted. But *peones* were digging in them, *gambesino*ing out the impoverished ore and pulverizing it in stone arrastras. The risks were terrible, but so was poverty. It was Hobson's choice: the mines assassinated them, poverty sentenced them to short lives of starvation and disease.

The Yaquis were not much better off. But they had the rich lands of the Yaqui River Valley in which to grow abundant crops, and when they needed cash, they raided a Mexican Army pay-train. Since the Mexican governors insisted on making war on them, the Indians found ways to use war as a crop, harvesting guns and pay-trains. Unfortunately, such a crop required blood for irrigation.

He entered the village, a concentration of *jacales* and even more primitive structures in the brush and trees, all of them with corrugated iron roofs stolen from old mine buildings. Some of the shacks looked like the kind children might build—rows of poles, door frames without doors, windows without glass, some houses without roofs. Dogs barked and the horse shied, kicking at them.

Fidel shouted at a boy and flipped him a peseta. *"Ándele decir a los Fröck qu'el gringo está aquí! Apúrete!"*

He reined in at the cantina, a small ruin with adobe walls from which most of the plaster had cracked, so that it resembled a hog from whose flanks dried mud was flaking. He left a boy to hold his horse and went inside. The cantina was dirt-floored, with a couple of very small square tables painted yellow, and a funnel attached to a hose in one wall. This was a urinal, close to the bar for the convenience of *borrachos*.

He bought two bottles of beer and sat down at a table with a sigh. He pulled off his spurred boots; his feet were hot. He had not eaten since breakfast, and it was nearly seven. In a few minutes Ricardo Fröck, the son of the family, appeared. He was dusty, as though he had come straight from some mine carcass he was picking.

They shook hands, and Fidel gave him the second beer. Ricardo was about twenty-five, with curly brown hair and a lined and pallid face.

"Where are your wagons?" he asked, in accented English.

"I didn't bring any this trip. My partner and I split up. I'm here on other business."

"I see." Ricardo smiled. "Some Yaquis raided the dance-hall in La Ventana last week. They are very bold, coming so far nort'."

"Was anyone hurt?"

"No. They never kill anyone but soldiers, or spies. They make everyone take off their clothes, and continue dancing!"

Fidel smiled. "Have they visited La Barranca lately?"

"No. But you never know when they come. They don't bother us. They come in maybe and help demselves to some mescal."

83

Fidel relaxed, finished the bottle of warm beer and went to the bar to get two more. The German's use of the word "mescal" meant a message had been brought to Ricardo, whose mother had thereupon hung her white apron on the clothesline. Then a Yaqui in the hills near La Barranca would know it was time to come down and talk to their friend, Fidel.

They finished their drinks and walked to the ramshackle home of the Fröcks. A boy led Fidel's horse. The various separate rooms of the house climbed the hillside. Chickens came and went in all of them except the *salón,* where Ricardo's mother was ironing a shirt with a charcoal iron. Her husband, who was blind, was already in bed. Mrs. Fröck was lean, brown as a Mexican, although she was European. She spoke in rapid-fire bursts of Spanish while setting the table.

"And how is your business, Don Gary?"

"Así, así."

"You have come without wagons."

"This time." Fidel used a handkerchief to fend off the flies trying to settle around his mouth and eyes. The woman shook her head.

"I am so sorry about the flies. It was not like this in Germany."

"It will be winter soon," said Fidel.

. . . He did not follow up on the remark about Germany, because Ricardo did not permit it. They had come to Hermosillo on some delusionary mining venture fifteen years ago, when he was a child; it had fallen apart, her husband went blind, and finally they had found their way here, where Ricardo worked the old mines for enough gold to feed them. Their story was a nightmare Fidel himself had when he thought about going broke, being devoured by debt, working as a miner until he gave out. Thinking of living in squalor like this, he wished he had killed John the other night.

He always felt guilty and apprehensive when he visited the family. The reason was clearer to him now than it had been: They represented, to a struggler like him, what was ahead when the roof fell in. A bare living, at best, sifting old mine dumps and risking your life in crumbling mines.

They ate a meal of beans, fried rice, and the big papery tortillas of Sonora, almost as large as a barrel-top. The beans had gone a little sour, and Fidel hoped for the best. He was too hungry to be choosy. He spread his blankets in a corner of Ricardo's bedroom. In doing so, he uncovered the sticks of dynamite he had brought, and presented them to Ricardo. They would save him many days of dangerous digging in the old tunnels.

After Mrs. Fröck had gone to bed, they sat up sipping tequila and chewing limes. They were killing time, waiting for a man to come to the doorless doorway, unannounced. Ricardo liked to talk about his version of religion. He was a free-thinker who believed in a supreme deity who was a sort of machine.

"It care nothing about people," he said. "But it care

about universal order. Often I have doubts. But one day I say, All right, we put you to test, if you are really somet'ing or no. If you show me where is ore wort' one hundred grams to d' kilo, maybe I believe."

Fidel was raising his glass when the night sounds of the village were dampened faintly; dogs were barking, a child crying, but the sounds suddenly lessened. He looked at the doorway. Someone was standing just outside in the dark. He had laid his Colt in his lap some time ago, in case one of Hogan's men came.

"*Amigo?*" he said.

"*Eh-wee,*" a man's voice said.

"*Pásele,*" Fidel said.

The man who entered, carrying a rifle, was too tall, too dark, to be Mexican. He wore a dark shirt with a neckerchief tied around the throat, baggy gray pants, and a small straw sombrero. The rifle was a bolt-action Mauser like Fidel's. He carried a small black memorandum book in his shirt pocket, because Yaquis did not believe in word-of-mouth messages. Bandoliers were crossed over his collarless shirt.

Ricardo poured him a glass of tequila and went outside to stand guard. Fidel turned down the wick of the coal oil lamp until only a sickroom illumination was left.

"What news?" the man asked. His name was Alejandro.

"I'm sorry. Still no gun."

"*When?*" the Yaqui hissed.

Fidel thumped the table. "I don't know, damn it! I

fought with my partner this week, but the gun is still mine. I have an idea," he said suddenly. "I'll sell it to you for five thousand dollars, *oro*, where it lies. Because I still have no idea how to smuggle it in."

Alejandro's dark, polished eyes regarded him steadily. "No," he said. "We buy it here. You bring it in by night?" he suggested. "East of Nogales?"

Fidel shook his head. "The Rurales are as thick as lice. Our train was stopped twice today. A soldier asked why I needed so much ammunition. I said for hunting. He didn't notice that the ammunition was wrong for my rifle. A good thing, eh? You see, I take risks for you, but this one has to be done exactly right."

"When?"

"I told you. I don't know when."

"Why did you come without freight?" asked the Indian.

"Because my partner lost half of our money. I have to have money to pay for it."

"Then why did you come at all?" Alejandro stayed alive by being suspicious.

"Because I had already sent you the message to meet me. And I have another errand, in La Ventana. Here—I'll fill your bandoliers."

The Yaqui removed them—they were almost empty—and he and Fidel emptied his own bandoliers and pushed the shells into the Yaqui's belt-loops. Now and then Alejandro would go outside and look around.

When the job was finished, they looked at each other.

"I'm sorry," Fidel said. "I need the money, you need the gun. I have your gunsmith, now—one who knows the gun and speaks Cáhita. If I should bring him and the gun next time, will your man be here?"

"Yes. But I am losing confidence in you."

"The gun weighs a hundred kilos!" Fidel argued. "And there is the carriage on top of that."

"General Valverde is encamped near Alamo. His force is growing every month. They are training. Our plans are made. We will retreat to—never mind where—and will ambush them, as usual. But to make them remember the lesson, we need the automatic gun. We will pile them up like rabbits and chase the survivors all the way to the railroad, as long as the gun lasts. Then we will have the Gatling guns they leave behind. We believe they have two. Once we learn to service the weapon, and have the ammunition they leave behind, we will be in a strong position for several years."

Fidel kept nodding, partly with fatigue, which was not helped by his sense of frustration. "I understand. . . . I will try hard. I need the money as much as you need the gun."

Alejandro reached in his pocket and brought out some golden coins. He placed them like checkers on the table. They looked newly minted.

"There will be hundreds of these when we get the gun," he said. "As it stands, here are two for the ammunition."

Fidel refilled the glasses. He felt very tired and slightly

drunk. *"Gracias,"* he said. *"Salúd y pesetas. . . ."*
"Y miles de rifles!"

Fidel lay awake for a half-hour, hectored by his old obsession with guns buried in corn meal, lard, mining machinery, and pickle brine. But nothing would work, nothing, nothing. . . . And soldiers going through trains was something new.

And when he had to give up on it, he would be forced to take a job in one of the mines, a boss maybe, rather than a miner, until Fidel's luck ran out again.

15

IN THE EARLY MORNING, it was cool and clear. Hearing Ricardo dressing, Fidel roused himself on the straw pallet where he had slept. He groaned with fatigue and anxiety. He heard sounds of children, barking dogs, tinkling goat bells, chickens in the yard. The air was perfumed with mesquite smoke. He washed up in the courtyard, and after looking at his battered, unshaven features in the broken mirror hung against a tree, took the time to shave. Today he might have to talk to a *padre* at the church about retrieving Allie's *milagro.* He did not want the priest to think he was merely a small-scale plunderer.

He ate some tortillas and *huevos rancheros,* drank some bitter black chicory coffee, paid for the family's services to him, and saddled his horse. It was a three-hour ride on up the mountain to La Ventana. He had two barrels of foodstuffs on the platform at Nogales for the small store in La Barranca. He stopped on the way out to explain to the *patrón* that he would bring them next time.

Riding up the mountain, he visited three small mines where he sold supplies. The *jefes* were stern, but gave him orders for additional materials, as well as lectures on reliability.

Late in the morning he rode into La Ventana, an old mining town just under the backbone of the mountains. From the plaza there was a view of scalloped ranges fading back into pearly blueness, in the direction of the state of Chihuahua. Big, bare and uneven, the red-earthed square was formed by mud-fronted buildings protected by arcaded walks. Horses, wagons, and oxcarts moved along the streets bounding the plaza, and people talked under the chinaberry trees.

The church, of plastered adobe, rose on the east, as arresting as a lighthouse. Three stories high, it presented a blank wall punctured with tall windows, with an elaborate central portion of carved pink stone. The two bell towers had small round roofs like the lids of Dutch ovens. Behind the church was a high-walled cemetery with broken glass copings.

The air was warm but not hot, pure as brook water, since there was no refinery to poison it here, as there was at Cananea and the northern mines. Here people existed by sifting old mine tailings and burrowing in crumbling tunnels, then working out the gold flakes in arrastras. Now and then the air pulsed to an explosion, as a charge was set off in a mine. The few big mines still operating paid their workmen eight pesos a day, starvation wages.

He climbed a few steps to the open door of the church, and entered. The interior was dim and cool, perfumed with scented candles. Rows of wooden benches stepped back to a raised altar. Religious pictures dating from Colonial times hung on the walls at each side. Behind the altar was a painted wooden statue of Santa Elena de Arizpe, with racks of candles burning before her and a framed wooden wallboard in the apse behind.

He wondered whether a service had been held here for Bernard Denis. A long way from Paris to be buried! The roads we travel, he sighed. But all roads led to a *campo santo* somewhere. Churches make me maudlin, he realized. He almost had tears in his eyes.

He climbed two steps to the raised section, gazed at the minor saints in the transepts left and right, at Santa Elena gazing sadly at him from dead ahead. He had always taken a bittersweet pleasure in reading the *milagros* and little memorial plaques in Mexican churches. Anything you needed to know about animals, Indians, and human frailty was recorded in them.

"Killed by a bear. Slain by the Indians. In the third year of her life, our little saint. . . ."

There were framed photographs with memorial statements beneath them, religious pictures, paper flowers, metal plaques sacred to the memory of . . .

Pedro Beas Ybarra. Falleció en La Ventana abril 4, 1834.

Falleció meant expired.

Ausención Villalobos. Falleció on Altar, enero 13, 1856.

María de la Cruz Villalobos. Murió a Horcasitas, Son. Nov. 27, 1876.

Juan Arvisu. Falleció en Nogales, A. T., marzo 11, 1895.

Dolores Riveroll vda de Morales. . . .

Something curious here; but what? A thread began unraveling in his mind. He shrugged and moved along to the hundreds of little silver *milagros* pinned to the saint's scoreboard—silver limbs, feet, hands, heads, hearts, lungs, livers, and lights. Many of them were large enough to be engraved, *Gracias, Sta. Elena.* His glance roved on, alert as a miner's for the shine of gold. He checked out some small offerings of gold— a hand, an eye, a foot. No heart of gold. But Bernard, according to Allie had had a heart of gold, alive as well as dead.

"Thou seek something?" said a voice, lisping in Castilian Spanish. He had been noticing a strengthening odor of liniment, and now realized it emanated from the black-robed priest behind him.

He turned, smiling, glad he had removed his sombrero. "How do you do, Padre? Yes, I am looking for a *milagro* dedicated to Santa Felicitas de Nogales. A friend—Bernard Denis, a Frenchman. . . ."

"Ah, *sí,* I recall. I am sorry, my friend, but it is not here."

"Oh? Well, do you happen to know—"

"The widow," said the priest. "The widow has it. She prefers to wear it, since it is not dedicated to our saint, as you know."

Fidel frowned. "The widow? No, no, you see she asked me if I would—" Then Fidel blinked, and put on the brakes. A light went on in his head. "I see," he said, nodding. "Of course. I thought I might say hello to her, since I knew Señor Denis quite well, in Nogales. I wonder where I'd find her?"

The priest cleared his throat, seeming embarrassed. ". . . Her name is Estella Nava viuda de Denis. I believe you'll find her in Calle de las Reyendas."

Bernard always knew where to find a good time. The name of the street meant Street of the Laughing Women. Fidel reached in his pocket, sorting through American and Mexican coins and settling on a small goldpiece, out of some intuition that he might need the *padre's* help before he was safely out of the Calle de las Reyendas. He handed him a twenty-peso piece Alejandro had given him last night. The priest thanked him and insisted on showing him some of the primitive art treasures of the church before he left.

16

UNDER A SKY THE clear blue of Indian turquoise, the *campo santo* behind the church looked ancient and disheveled. The aisles wandered drunkenly, the ground was irregular, the stones were a jumble of every size and type. Padre Severo had explained how to find Bernard's grave. It was tucked into the southeast corner, near a silver-fenced family grouping. He started his search.

The stone markers and statues were black with age; the black marble slabs shone. On many of the graves rested glass jars which had turned amethyst from the assault of hot suns, some containing real or paper flowers, others empty, or overturned. Some graves were adorned with silver bosses, or chains, while more modest slabs consisted of nothing but illegible names chiseled into soft stone.

He found the iron-clad earth of the Hassenfratz family; an unlikely name for Mexico, but not so unusual as it might seem to a first-time visitor to a Mexican graveyard. The Germans, he had noticed, were great colonizers. Assuming this was the plot the priest had meant—nine children under two years of age slept here—the Frenchman should be buried nearby. He took a sighting, and saw an iron stake, painted gray, with a small metal case bolted to it. He walked to the grave and looked down.

The earth was still swollen in a rectangular shape where the coffin had been interred. The widow—or someone—had laid on it a red cactus blossom, in a jar. It had wilted to a puddle of red petals. Inside the box, which had a small glass window, was a card bearing a name and number, and the sepia photograph of a man.

Going to one knee, he studied the picture.

It was Bernard, all right. He looked dashing and

keen, with healthy gray hair and a black General Grant beard. He wore a boiled collar and a satin tie with a diamond in it. His name was on the card, and the statement: *A citizen of La Ventana, Son.*

Was there any point in pursuing the matter? Well, yes, if Allie was determined to hang that *milagro* on Santa Teresita's scoreboard. Would the Mexican widow give it up? Probably not very happily. But maybe he could buy it.

He leaned against the high adobe wall and pondered. However he explained it, Allie was in for a shock. She wanted the votive offering, as well as his personal effects. And she had hinted that she would like the body brought home on one of his trips.

If he went back with empty hands, and a lame story, would she suspect the truth? Well, why should he care? Yet somehow he did. He didn't give a damn about Bernard's reputation—let him pay the piper, dead or not—but he didn't want Allie hurt. If he went to the Street of the Laughing Women, it would be to protect her, and, just possibly, to strengthen his hand with her.

He gazed around the dead acre of dirt and stone, frowning. If he failed to bring back the heart, she might want the body brought back. Might anyway, with her exaggerated feelings about the old Frenchman. He pictured himself directing a gravedigger in the exhumation, loading it onto a wagon. The vision was distasteful and ridiculous.

But then a bell rang in his head, summarily, as in a

mine when the elevator was about to descend. Attention!

A run of gooseflesh went up his arms. A coffin could carry a lot of things—a gun as well as a dead man! But, wait a minute. The coffin would be going the wrong way: north.

Well, suppose he bought a coffin in Nogales and freighted it down here to return the Frenchman in? Fine idea—except that the customs inspector would have it opened to see what he was smuggling into Sonora.

No, Bernard, he sighed, you weren't any use to me alive, and you're no more use dead.

From a corner of the plaza a rutted street sloped a few blocks south. There were ancient stone curbs but no sidewalks, potholes brimming with muddy water from a summer rain, skinny dogs, windowless walls, a few dark-leaved Indian laurels casting a generous shade but tearing up the curbs. He dismounted before a cantina where a couple of pulque drunkards slept on the walk, snot running down their faces; someone was playing a guitar inside. *The Gates of Hell* the sign over the door read. Close enough, thought Fidel. He stepped into the cool, sour smell of pulque, the milky drink that enabled the impoverished to endure their lives.

"Calle de Las Reyendas," he said to the man behind the bar.

"Mas allá," the man said, gesturing. *"Un cuadro."*

Fidel walked the horse to the next corner. In daylight

The Street of the Laughing Women resembled any other street. He rode on, alert for signs of life. A girl about ten peeked out of an open door, thin and dirty. Fidel called to her.

"Estella Nava?" he said.

"Sí, señor."

"Does she live here?"

"No, señor."

"Well, can you show me?" He held up a peso. The girl ran out, took the coin, and started down the street. He rode after her. A half-block south she knocked on the frame of an open door.

"Here," she said. *"Viuda de Denis."* She ran off.

A young woman came to the door. She was hardly more than a girl, scarcely five feet tall, and looked remarkably like Allie Denis. Her hair was dark, brushed back and caught with a barrette, before falling below her shoulders. Her floor-length dress was lime-green, and she was barefoot. She smiled at him, revealing a gold tooth. Her fingers toyed with a gold necklace she wore, at the end of which he saw a gold heart that resembled a Valentine gift. Fidel smiled back and swung down. He was aware of other women's heads at other doors.

She backed into the house, inviting him inside. Her fingers were already working with the top button of her dress. He took off his hat at the doorway but shook his head.

"Excuse me, señora," he said. "This is in regard to my business, not yours. I will pay you double for your time."

97

"What are you up to?" the little woman said, frowning in suspicion.

"I was a friend of your husband's, in Nogales."

"Well? What do you want?"

Fidel sat on the only chair in the room; the woman lay on her elbow on the rumpled bed. "I would like to buy the *milagro* you're wearing."

"It's not for sale. Only me." She giggled waiting for him to decide.

Ways and means, schemes, plots and subterfuges dodged through his mind. But, after a prolonged, awkward pause, he arrived at nothing better than the truth. He sighed.

"I knew your husband's American wife, too," he said.

She shook her head. "He had no wife in America," she said. "I was married to him for over a year before he died. All that time he was right here in La Ventana. Except for little business trips to Nogales."

"I don't mean to insult the memory of the dead," he said, "but let me show you something. This is his diploma from an engineering school in France. And this is his birth certificate. His widow gave them to me to show the padre. She wants me to bring back the gift he promised Santa Teresita de Nogales."

He saw her glance at a picture on the wall: Bernard. In an open cupboard, a man's gray suit, piped with black, hung from a hook. The woman began to cry. He kept telling her he was sorry, he would pay for the *milagro,* but when she looked up, wiping her eyes with both palms, she said,

"No. It's not for sale. He wouldn't want her to have it. He was so good to me. We lived well—I didn't have to do this before. Or at least—not after I married him. No, she can't have it; she can't have anything, the bitch."

"He was a citizen of the Estados Unidos," Fidel said sternly, hoping to scare her.

"Pooh," she said. "He was a citizen of France."

"The widow would like me to bring his body back some day. He had a home there. It's only right that he should go home. . . . His priest told me he was hoping the *milagro* would be returned, too."

The girl's dark eyes challenged him. "Who was his priest?"

Thank God Allie had told him! "Padre Abelardo."

He saw in her shrug that he had scored one small point. "But how about me?" Estella pouted. "What would I have left of him? The bitch gets the body and the heart of gold."

"At least you wouldn't have to pay rent on his grave. If it isn't paid, his bones go into a common grave, you know that. All right, I'll pay you a hundred pesos, gold, when you give me your permission. Take some time to think about it. I can't do it yet, anyway."

The girl said: "The woman would have to come here and ask. On her knees." She pointed at the dirt floor.

"Why?" he argued. "Come on, Estella—"

She laughed. "Everything has a price. That's the

price. How many Mexican women get to see an American woman on her knees?"

Fidel gazed at the rip-rap ceiling. It was a hell of a time for a woman to come down here; or for a trader, as far as that went. But she might have to, if the plan he was putting together, on a sudden, almost mystical hunch, were to work.

"All right. I understand. Where did you meet Bernard?" he asked.

Estella went to a scarred dresser and picked up a man's silver hairbrush. She removed the barrette, let her hair fall free, and began to brush it.

"In my aunt's house. I was fifteen. He took me to a little house he rented. I lived like a queen."

Fifteen, Fidel thought. Bernard liked to pick them green and let them ripen. For some reason he had a distasteful vision of Allie, much younger, standing in an open door beckoning at men on the street. *No, no: impossible.* Then, *Don't be a dreamer:* he thought, *it had to be something like this.*

He said goodbye and started out, then came back. He dug some coins from his pocket.

"How much do I owe you?" he asked.

"Ten pesos."

He put them on the dresser. "You met him at your aunt's, you said. Was she a *puta,* too?"

"Of course. My mother, also. But she died, and I went to live with my aunt."

"I see. . . ."

She regarded him with a blend of amusement and

contempt. "What's the difference?"

"I just wondered."

"Men always want to know why. Why not, hombre? Thirty-three centavos a day working in the fields. Thirty pesos a night here. Still, it was like a dream with Bernardo. *Ay de mi!* At least I refuse to kiss them."

17

HOW HAD THE MEMORIAL plaque in the church been phrased?

As he rode back, he tried to remember the words, but all he recalled were: *Nogales, A. T., 1895.* Fidel believed in a level of his mind deeper than thought, beyond control; but one that, given enough time, often supplied answers to questions. He had been letting it solve the problem of smuggling the Gatling gun, but it had disappointed him. Maybe he had tried too hard. It was difficult to express what he thought, but in a way his belief was like that of Ricardo's, in a divine machine which ran men's affairs. Now, it seemed, it was putting together an answer for him.

He tied the horse before the church and removed his hat as he strode up the steps. Entering the scented dusk, he looked around for the padre. He did not see him, and walked forward, spurs chiming.

"Padre? Father Severo—?"

He was approaching the altar when the priest stepped into view from a door off the transept, at the right. "Yes. Did you find the woman?"

"I did. We talked about my taking the body of Señor Denis back to the States. You see—this won't surprise a man of your experience with mortal failings—he was married to another woman in San Francisco, five years ago! She now lives in Nogales. Are you the one who married him and Estella Nava?"

"I did. May God forgive him." Padre Severo made the sign of the cross, and liniment fumes wafted to Fidel's nostrils.

"The other widow may want to return his body to Nogales," Fidel said. "He would be reinterred in holy ground at the church of Santa Felicitas. Would that be acceptable to the church here?"

"I expect so."

"I know she would want to pay for any trouble she put the church to. Oh, and—while I'm here—" Fidel gazed at the wall where the *milagros* and plaques were fixed. "I remember a La Ventana man—I forget the name—who died in Nogales last year. Do you recall him?"

The priest walked toward the shadowed apse. "Juan Arvisu, a miner. I said a memorial service for him, last—I forget exactly when. But here is the plaque."

Fidel restrained himself from pounding the priest on the back. And in any case, the matter was still not entirely settled. Arms hanging, holding his hat by the brim, he read the words his mind had fished up for him.

"A miner," he sighed. "A poor man, of course. I was

102

a miner, too. I suppose he had walked to Arizona to make a little more money at his trade."

"That is usually the reason.

"And he lies in the *campo santo* there?"

"*Como no!* What miner's widow has the money to bring her man home?"

Fidel gestured, smiling. "You see, *padre,* as I was riding back to talk to you, I had an idea. Why not have a coffin made in Nogales—the one I'll be taking Denis home in? I'll be bringing in a couple of wagon loads of freight anyway. If I do that, I could bring Arvisu's body back to his widow. I would be glad to pay for a mass for him here. Is his widow still in town?"

"She lives a couple of kilometers from here, but I'll speak to her when she comes in for mass on Sunday. I am sure she'll be grateful."

Fidel felt as though ants were crawling in his veins. He smiled his gratitude, too broadly, probably, and offered his hand. "Thank you, Father. Now I'm going to eat at that little restaurant down the street—El Sonorense—and come back afterward for a letter from you. I expect the customs people will want something, at the border."

"I don't know. But I'll write a letter asking them to permit you to bring the body into Mexico. . . ."

As he walked to the restaurant, Fidel caught himself kicking a small cobblestone along the walk like a soccer ball. Just keep the damned Rurales out of my way, he thought. I'll have that Gatling gun in La Barranca next week!

103

It was an easy ride downhill to La Barranca after lunch, the letter from the priest in his pocket. There would be enough daylight, even, to hang Mrs. Fröck's apron on the clothesline to summon Alejandro from wherever he hid out in the brush and silk-trees above the village. The fragments of his plan were coalescing in his mind like droplets of mercury.

Approaching the village, he thought of a little refinement that made him chuckle. Candles! He would buy or borrow a set of church candelabra to place on the coffin when he brought it across! Everything was so easy, now. Why had the solution eluded him for so long? The cemetery in Nogales was probably half-full of Mexican miners, any one of whom he could have brought home to some widow or other, along with Alejandro's gun.

A hundred yards from the Fröck's ramshackle home, as he jogged down the red ruts, he saw a horseman and a man afoot in the road. Ice water poured through his bowels. The man afoot wore the conventional baggy gray of the Mexican soldier. The other was clad in a gray uniform with silver buttons and braid and a loose red necktie. An officer, by God! So there had to be a detachment here, probably camping in town!

He thought, with dismal acceptance of the catastrophe, that it had been too easy. Nothing was ever that easy. Not in Fidel's world.

18

THE OFFICER WAS A lieutenant of Rurales, Teniente Lopez. He was younger than Fidel, and in excellent physical condition, like most Rurales, soldiers who had an Indian's ability to live on the land and ride or walk until they got there. Seated on his horse a couple of yards from him, Fidel studied his unsmiling face. He looked proud, lynx-like, sober; nobody's fool, in short. Fidel wondered whether he had been in on the Indian-hanging last year, when four Yaquis were strung up from a telegraph pole beside the railroad tracks.

"Your name, gringo? Your business?"

"I'm a trader, Teniente, Gary Fidel."

"What do you trade?" The lieutenant's eyes appraised him like a horse he was planning to buy, checking out his clothing, his mount, his weapons. The soldier stood idly with his rifle resting on the road.

"Mining machinery and cattle."

"Where are your wagons?"

"No wagons this time. I went to La Ventana to do a favor for a friend in Nogales. Her husband is buried in the *campo santo* there. I spoke to Padre Severo about permission to move his body home. I have his letter in my pocket." He patted the pocket of his jacket.

"Where are you going now?"

"To the house of Señora Fröck, to spend the night."

The officer leaned forward and reached toward Fidel's rifle. *"Con permiso—"* He pulled the Mauser from the boot and examined it, then smiled at Fidel. "Stolen from the Mexican Army."

"Possibly. It was sold to me by a man in Arizona last year."

"Are you sure it was not an Indian?"

"Positive. Would a Yaqui sell a gringo a gun?"

"Nevertheless, in Mexico it is illegal for a civilian to possess government arms. I'm confiscating it."

The lieutenant tossed the weapon to the soldier, who caught it with one hand, and grinned at Fidel. He was a harelip, as dark as the seat of a saddle.

"I won't arrest you, but be careful next time. Pass."

"Has there been some trouble here, Teniente?"

"No. We're billeted here at the moment."

For how long? Where? How many soldiers? He dared not ask. But he said: "Is there room for me at the Fröcks', or is someone billeted there?"

"There is room."

When he reined in before the Fröck place, which resembled a collection of mud-and-wattle hen-houses climbing the hillside, he saw some laundry on the clothesline sagging between two mesquite trees. At the right end of it was a faded red shirt. Red, in that position, was a message to the Indians to stay away. But Fidel, alarm ringing in him like a fire-bell, had a postscript to add to it.

Mrs. Fröck appeared, shooing chickens away with

her apron. "What news?" she asked, as he led his horse toward the spiny ocotillo-wand goat corral above the buildings.

"How many soldiers are there in the village?" he muttered.

"Six, as far as we know."

"Where is Ricardo?"

"He'll be coming from his arrastra soon."

"I'd like you to hang your apron next to the red shirt. Alejandro already knows there's danger—he probably knew it before you did. But I've got news for him. I'll pay extra for the risk."

The woman was already hanging up her apron. "All right," she said. "But I don't like this."

"I apologize," Fidel said, sincerely.

Ricardo tramped home from the mine, muddy with the pulverized ore he had been wading in all day. While he washed up in the yard, Fidel played the part of a weary trader, lounging in a leather-slung chair under a tree with a glass of tequila in his right hand and Mrs. Fröck's yellow-headed parrot on the index finger of his other hand. A soldier tramped by, with the ardor of a farmer following a plowhorse. The parrot said something that sounded like, tut-tut.

"His eyes turn orange when he talks," Fidel commented. "Why do you suppose that is?"

"Parrots' eyes have big pupils," said Ricardo, drying his chest on a gray towel. "They close down when he makes a sound, and show d' real color. Mine open big when I am scared. They are open now."

Fidel chuckled. "Mine too, I expect. I'll see if I can help your mother. . . ."

"She's all right." Ricardo lowered his voice. "Alejandro came to the mine. I don't like him to do that. He asked how many soldiers were in town, what they wanted. I couldn't tell him. He'd seen the signal."

"I hope he'll see the other."

Ricardo frowned when he saw the second message beside the first. "Is it wise, my friend?"

"Maybe not, but it's my only choice."

It was almost dark when they ate in the *zaguán,* the palm-covered breezeway between the kitchen and living room. It was a good dinner—fried chicken, rice, beans, and tomatoes. Fidel ate as though it might be his last supper, sipping tequila now and then. He was disciplining himself, preparing for a time not far ahead when the danger would be so much greater that tonight would be remembered with nostalgia. The parrot flapped to his shoulder and looked into his mouth to see what he was eating.

"Give him some cheese," said Mrs. Fröck, tight-lipped.

Fidel offered him a morsel of white goat-cheese, and the bird accepted it, with a ruffle of tail feathers.

"This is dangerous," Ricardo muttered.

"Yaquis can make themselves invisible. They've been ambushing Mexican soldiers for two hundred years. There was a famous battle in which the Yaquis clung to the offside of grazing cattle, and moved right into the Mexican line. Then they jumped off and massacred them all. Don't worry."

Ricardo looked at him and shuddered.

A pebble landed beside the truss table. The German frowned. He peered up the hill, dark now. "I hear the goats moving. Did you leave your horse in the corral?"

"Yes. I'd better check him."

As he had expected, Alejandro was waiting beside the corral, his rifle in his hands.

19

"I'LL NEED SEVEN DAYS," Fidel told the Indian. "It's all arranged here. But I've got a lot to do in Nogales."

He explained the plan. Alejandro's head kept turning like that of a hawk on the highest branch of a dead tree. "The gun won't be worth anything to us unless the gunsmith comes. Are you sure he speaks Cáhita? Our gunsmith speaks no Spanish."

"I'm sure. On the seventh day, I'll meet you wherever you say."

"Take the road to Rincon when you leave La Ventana. Someone will meet you beside the road. If it's dangerous, if there are *yoris* around, pretend you've lost a wheel. Work on it until you hear from us."

Yoris meant cry-babies, the Yaqui word for Mexican soldiers; but enough cry-babies at the right place could ruin even a Yaqui's plans.

"There will be a woman with me," he said. "God, I've got to find a way out of that! But I don't get the body unless the woman asks for it nicely, and without the body in the coffin, I'm dead if they stop me. So the woman will most likely be along."

"You shouldn't have made an arrangement like that," Alejandro said severely.

"Alejandro," Fidel said, "I'll bring you melons, or mining machinery, or pickles, any time you want, in any way you want. But when it comes to Gatling guns—I write my own shipping ticket. Seven days from tomorrow. If you don't see me then, be patient. Something unforeseen might come up."

"What about ammunition?"

"I'll cram in all I can. The gun has a drum magazine that holds four hundred cartridges. Each barrel will fire forty shots a minute, and there are ten barrels in the gun. So, theoretically, you can lay down a fire that would melt a fort."

"Eh-wee," said the Yaqui. "We have faced the gun. But it didn't have a drum. It had twenty-shot magazine. We've captured some, but can't make them work."

"This one is a later model. It will work when my friend gets through with it. How about the money?"

"It will be in four saddle-bags, Mexican gold. You can put it in the dead-box, I suppose, after the gun has been taken out."

It sounded like duck soup, Fidel thought, as he picked his way back down the hill, in the dark. Why didn't he go into it professionally? Well, I may be foolhardy, he thought, but I'm not crazy. And I'll be glad when this is over.

20

OLD ARTHUR WAS AT the depot to meet him. The sight of him, with his turkey-buzzard head and arresting nose was somehow reassuring. At least some things, like Arthur's Nose, never changed. He wore his decent black suit despite the dry, insistent heat of the early afternoon. He reached up for Fidel's suitcase, and Fidel tossed down his bedroll and gun-boot and carried his saddle off the train.

"Fine news, Mr. Fidel!" he said, as they walked toward the station. "A chance to lease a rendering plant!"

What's that got to do with me? Fidel thought wearily. But he remembered the conversation about hogs, lard, candles and soap.

"Good," he said. "Why don't you sit here in the shade while I go in and let Tom Hall know I'm back?"

"Certainly. Nice young man," Arthur added, wheezing. "I've talked to him about your, er, situation, since he moved in with us. I think he might just decide you're a good man to be in business with."

Fidel patted him on the shoulder; it felt like a wooden framework under the cloth. "I hope so. Thanks, Arthur."

Hall was taking down a message. He nodded at Fidel, tore a slip off the message pad and called his messenger. The old man came in and carried it away. Fidel leaned on the counter to rest his tired bones.

"Good trip?" asked Hall.

"Así, así." Fidel looked around to be sure they were alone. "Are you feeling up to another trip to the mine? I've got to move that machinery to my office and uncrate it."

"Tonight?"

"The sooner the better. Do you know if the lock's been changed on my office?"

Hall handed him a key from his desk.

"I'll be driving out in that little wagon of mine," Fidel said. "See you at supper."

Arthur went to the office with him, where he dumped the saddle, bedroll, and rifle-boot. It smelled stale and dusty in the room, and the heat was suffocating. But Arthur looked around as though it were Leo Lucas' office at the bank.

"This could be made very nice," he said. "You'd need a proper filing cabinet and a few things. I can't impress on you too strongly your need to diversify, Gary—"

"You did it!" Fidel exclaimed. "You called me Gary."

Arthur blushed. "You've been on my mind so much— all the ins and outs of your situation—I must be thinking of you as a son. If you *were* my son, I'd tell you to put down some money on that lease. The rendering plant hasn't been used in years, and I hear they're about to tear it down. I got old man Akins to hold up while you considered the matter. The rent is only thirty dollars a month—I've got all the figures at the house. . . ."

Fidel thought of what was ahead in Sonora, and compared it with the life of a soap-and-tallow man, with a sideline of hog-butchering. Compared to being hung from a telegraph pole it did not sound so bad. And actually, Arthur would do most of the work. It would be a paper-job. Paper was where the money was.

"I'll talk to Akins before I go back to La Ventana," he promised. "At the worst, I'll lose a couple of hundred. When I come back from Sonora next time, I'll either be able to afford anything, or it won't matter much what I get into. I'm going to have a drink at the hotel now, Arthur. Will you join me?"

"Thank you, Gary. I've had my drink for the day—a beer before lunch. Drat it, it made me wheeze."

Buzzing slightly with a double shot of whiskey, Fidel lay in the zinc tub, soaking out the worries and the stiffness, while trying to think of possible ways to phrase an impossible statement. Allie had to know about the other woman; yet how could he tell her? And wouldn't it all lead directly to the unavoidable truth of where Allie herself had come from? All the birds in her life. Even the witnesses at her marriage had been birds! Did that somehow explain the perpetual vow of mourning, the black garments, the long sleeves?

It had to be brought out, between the two of them, if only because she had to go to La Ventana with him. He had worried that she might insist on accompanying Bernard's body back to Nogales; but that, of course, was out of the question. There was a stagecoach she could take from La Ventana to the railroad. That dilemma, at least, was settled.

But what if her love for Bernard went out like a candleflame—as it ought to—when she learned about Estella? If she wouldn't come along, he probably could not get the body out of the ground. In that case, he would have no cover for the gun.

She had to go with him.

And she must tell him about San Francisco. I can handle it now, he thought. There's a good explanation. She was only, what—? fifteen? A good girl who—his thoughts thickened like mud, gloom filled him.

A knocking on the door made him start. He had fallen asleep in the cooling water. "All right," he called. "Five minutes."

It was five-thirty when he left the hotel barber shop. He smelled like Johnny Hogan, he suspected—bay rum, whiskey, and cigar smoke. But he was clean, and the claw-marks on his face were healing.

No one was sitting on the porch but Arthur, who spoke quickly. "There's another way you could—"

"Will it keep, Arthur? I've got something to tell Allie."

"Of course, of course! I'll mull it over some more."

A delightful fragrance welcomed him to the cool entry. A stew? And certainly some of Bare-nar's Formula coffee. "Allie?" he called.

"In the kitchen! Gary?"

She was fussing with a couple of dozen objects on the drainboard, a long white apron covering her from neck to shins. They rested on a flat baking pan, and resembled large, cheap terra-cotta marbles sprinkled with chopped parsley.

She faced him, fists on hips. "You've been gone a week!" she accused.

"Four days."

"Couldn't you have come here straight from the station? I heard that you came in this afternoon. Arthur said—"

"I've been drinking, Allie. And sleeping. Getting a shave and thinking." He nodded at the objects on the baking pan. "What are those things?"

She draped a towel over them. *"Escargots,"* she said. "I promised to make them sometime, you know. They're to celebrate your safe return."

She studied his face, frowning but excited, almost girlish. "What is it?" she said. "You look unhappy. The *milagro?* Couldn't you find it?"

"I found it. Around the neck of a little woman who could have been you, except that she was even smaller."

Allie's lips parted. "What are you telling me, Gary?" she asked, her voice pitched low. "Why wasn't it in the church?"

"I wish I didn't have to tell you this," he said. "A man—that is, living away from his wife for long periods—"

"He had a woman," she said flatly, appearing less shocked than he had anticipated.

"He had a wife, Allie. His Mexican widow is wearing the heart now."

She sat down on a straight-backed chair and laid her hands in her lap. Without looking very broken up, she was crying. Her tears flowed painlessly, effortlessly, bountifully, down her cheeks. Although she was biting her lip, she looked as though she enjoyed the weeping. He went to lay his hand on her shoulder, patting it affectionately.

"Don't think too bad of him," he murmured. "He was still a very good man. But lonesome."

She sniffled. He handed her his blue bandana. "Of course he was a good man," she said, her voice muffled. "A wonderful man."

"Do you want his body back, to sleep in the churchyard of his favorite saint? Do you want the *milagro?*"

She wiped her eyes. "Yes, of course. Well, but—what did she say?"

Fidel looked around, wishing there were some cooking sherry on the drainboard that he could sip for fortification. All he saw was a bottle of vinegar with herbs drowned in it.

"She was as surprised to hear about you as you were about her. But she was fairly cooperative."

"Fairly?"

"She'll let me bring the body back, and she'll sell us the *milagro*. On certain conditions. . . ."

"I can imagine," Allie said, with a note of coldness. "What are they?"

"You'll have to ask her. In person. But that's not too bad, is it?"

". . . No. Not too bad. We'd both get something, so

it would be a fair contract. She'd get revenge, I'd get his remains, and the heart. When?"

"As soon as I can get a coffin made, and make some arrangements. Day after tomorrow; maybe the day after that."

He decided not to mention the body they would be freighting to La Ventana. Why complicate things at this point?

Allie sighed. "What kind of woman is she? As if I didn't know," she added, with a brief laugh.

Fidel walked to the sink, peering out the window across the smoky evening town. He gestured vaguely. "She's, um—no worse, no better, than you'd expect. . . ."

"A fancy woman?"

He cleared his throat, scratched his scalp. "Why do you say that?"

"Just a hunch—a *soupçon,* as Bernard used to say. Is she?"

"Yes. Of course, things are pretty well regulated in Mexico, when it comes to love matters. He'd have had to court a, you know, decent—no, no, let's say, *ordinary* woman, for a long time, make arrangements with her relatives and all that."

"Yes, I suppose. Things weren't so different in San Francisco when he married me, though, poor man. He wanted a wife, in a hurry. But he was very good to me, always."

"Yes. Well, that's the long and short of it Allie. If you're in agreement, I'll order the coffin made. Riley's Furniture—"

Allie rose and walked to his side. They looked out the window together. "I want to talk about it now. Now that I'm—nailed to the wall. I want to confess, as Bernard used to."

"I'm no priest, Allie! God! But I give you absolution here and now. Don't say a word."

"Have you ever been really poor?" she asked.

He barked. "My parents were Basque sheepherders in Oregon. I had sheepbones for playthings. I wore sheepskin and ate sheep till I ran away and discovered denim and beef. I was poor, yes. I'm still poor, if you mean not having more than a few hundred dollars in the bank."

"I mean poor the way you are in the city. I told you my father's name was Fitzgerald. Or did I say O'Brien? I forget which I used this time. Actually, I don't know what it was, nor who he was. And neither did my mother. She was a *fille de joie*."

"I guess I know that much French. But Allie—"

"Hush. Whatever she was, I was born to the trade. When I was fifteen, my mother decided I was old enough to start. I'd just started when Bernard came to her Bird House, as the police called it. All the girls had bird names. Mine was Blue Bird, or would have been. But Bernard fell in love with me on sight. He paid her something, and we were actually married, by a priest!"

"The cur," Fidel muttered.

"Why? He took me out of a terrible life, didn't he? How can you criticize a man who could make a decent, educated wife out of a—a young slut. Teach her grammar, as well as French. *'Je vous aime, tu m'aime, il l'aime. . . .'* I could go on. And not only that, but how to make a delicious morsel out of a garden snail."

Fidel shuddered. "Now, *that* is one of the worst things I ever heard about a Frenchman!"

Allie whipped the towel off the objects she had been working with when he entered the kitchen. He saw that they were clean, buttered garden snails flecked with parsley. "Allie!" he groaned. "My God! Are you trying to poison everybody?"

"They . . . are . . . delicious," she said decisively. "And if you want me to do what you have in mind, you'll have to do what I have in mind. I'll beg that woman to give me my husband's remains, and his amulet. But in return you'll have to do something for me."

"All right, Allie," Fidel said, frowning uneasily at the snails.

"You'll eat the first snail, and tell the others it's delicious."

"A raw insect?" he cried. "A—a slug?"

"I bake them, with garlic butter, and they resemble little bits of tenderloin. That's the first thing. And the second is that after we bury Bernard, you'll loan me the money to leave Nogales. I know why you fought Johnny Hogan, and I suppose everyone else, and his wife, knows it too. *En tout cos,* I couldn't fool people forever, if only because I can't stand wearing long sleeves much longer. Not in this heat."

"Why do you need to?"

She smiled wryly and began to unbutton the small pearl buttons on her left cuff. "Oh, you haven't caught on? I was sure you had, when you kept hinting that day about my wearing mourning forever, and my long sleeves."

She folded back the cuff. On her wrist, just where a doctor would take her pulse, a small bluebird was tattooed. ". . . It was so the customers would remember us. But now I've got it for the rest of my life. What man would marry a tattooed lady, Gary?"

She laughed, a bit shrilly. "The Tattooed Lady! I'll get a lot more tattoos! A cross and anchor, a gravestone with 'Mother' on it! A snake! I'll hire on with a circus! If you want to go with me, you can be the strong man."

"Hush!" Fidel groaned. "Marry me, Allie. We'll go away—"

He heard the mosquito-bar door squeak open. "You wouldn't stay with me long," she said, "after you'd had a few more fights over your tattooed wife. Forget it, Gary. I wouldn't do such a thing to someone I love. I have a little pride left—the pride Bernard gave me in myself, the pride I have that a man like you finds me lovable. . . ."

Fidel grabbed her in a bear hug, and she gasped. There were tears in his eyes. He was determined to crush the nonsense out of her, to force her to love and accept him. But she squirmed like a trout. Gaily she cried through the doorway:

120

"Tom? Sit yourself down. I'll bring you some sherry. We're celebrating Gary's return. *A merveille, non?*"

21

AT THE LIVERY STABLE, they were talking about Johnny Hogan. O'Brien, the furniture maker, was telling the story to a half-dozen men when Fidel and Tom walked in after dinner. It was dark, the stable lighted only in a small area in the front where a hung lantern was being assaulted by moths.

"So he says, 'Rub my head with your lodge ring, Bill, maybe it'll change my luck,'" O'Brien related. "I did, and he puts all he's got left on double zero. And that's what he got out with. Two times zero, which is still zero. Blew the whole wad!"

"This was my ex-partner?" Fidel asked, knowing they were all watching for his reaction.

"Old Jawn, yep. He brought in forty-fifty Mexican steers yesterday, dog-tired, and sold them to that fellow, Aguirre. He's dead beat, so he just gets drunk and goes to the hotel. But this afternoon he starts gambling."

"So he's broke," Fidel said. "What about his jewelry?"

"Oh, yes. That big gold thing, wrist-brace or whatever he calls it, so he won't have to call it a bracelet—it's on the Palace Saloon backbar. He'd already put it in hock to them. Buys it back last night, and loses it again today. The thing must weigh four pounds, stripped. He says he made it himself. Nice work, if he did. The Mexican eagle."

Fidel asked the liveryman to get his little delivery wagon ready. One horse would be enough. He was moving some machinery from the station to his office. As O'Brien walked to the door, Fidel called:

"Bill? I've got a job for you. I need a coffin."

The furniture man looked at him, suspecting a joke. "What for?"

"I'm taking the remains of a Mexican miner named Arvisu to La Ventana with me on my next trip. The padre put the arm on me when I was up there. He died in a cave-in last year, out at Oro Blanco."

"Yes, I remember. Nothing too fancy?"

"No, but not bargain basement, either. You see, after I unload Arvisu, I'm picking up Allie Denis's man, the Frenchman. What was his name?"

"Bare-*nar* Den-*ee*, he called himself," O'Brien grinned.

"That's the one, *Mercy bo-coop*, Bill. Say, listen. Could I pick it up tomorrow night? I'll be leaving the next day."

"Well, I wouldn't have time to paint it. I could stretch black cloth over it, if you like."

"Good, good. Make it look very funereal. His widow will love it. With a screw-on lid, so I won't have to dynamite it off in La Ventana, okay?"

He and Tom drove out in the direction of the railroad station. But at the tracks, they turned north and headed out of town.

122

They were back in three hours, silent and tired. They halted in the alley behind Fidel's office, and he went around and unlocked the door. With the blinds drawn, they opened the crate. Hall worked eagerly, laying out the ten barrels of the gun, the crank, the plate and casing, and wiping them clean of cosmoline. He checked out the appendages—wrenches and screw drivers and clamps. Everything was there, even a drum magazine.

"I'd like to put this thing together and just see —"

"Can't risk it, Tom," Fidel said. "This goes in the desk until we're ready to leave. I've got to buy shells, too. Maybe you'd better buy up a few boxes of forty-five cartridges for me, so I won't look too ridiculous buying all the ammunition in the store."

"You're right." Hall peered at him. "Fidel, I hope you realize a gun like this can't be fired by one man holding it and another cranking it? It's a field piece, really—weighs a hundred and forty pounds. It's got to have a carriage. Have you got one? If so, how are we going to ship it?"

"You rode on it tonight," Fidel said. "The front wheel assembly of my wagon. That's why it's such a little wagon, with such a clumsy tongue. We'll carry the coffin on it, and when we unload in the mountains, we lift off the wagon bed and there's your carriage—the front wheels! We mount the gun on the carriage, and the Indians take off. They could pull it by hand, or with a horse if they've got one."

"Then what do we do for a wagon to get back to Villa Camargo?"

"I'll wire Gardea that I need one. We'll go up to La Ventana with two wagons, and leave what's left of mine behind. Tomorrow O'Brien will make that coffin, and I'll make the arrangement to have Arvisu exhumed. Next day I'll have him dug up. But we'll load the gun into the coffin tomorrow night, as soon as it's ready. —Let's have a nightcap and go to bed."

In the morning he went up to the old church, in a little canyon off the road to Tucson. He showed Father Abelardo the letter from the curate in La Ventana.

"The widow is a very poor woman," he said. "I want to pay for the exhumation and any other charges myself."

The priest was a middle-aged man with a yellow-brown face, lined and rather jaded. He moved his lips as he read the letter, then nodded. "That would be all right. Are you a Catholic, by the way?"

"No, but I have the greatest respect." Fidel pulled an ear-lobe. "I was wondering—would it be a good thing to burn candles on the casket at night? We'll be on the road a couple of days."

"It couldn't hurt." Father Abelardo smiled at this rather touching naiveté.

"I'll buy something across the line—some nice copper candelabra. O'Brien is making the coffin today. I plan to pick up the body tomorrow morning, in time to catch the morning train to Camargo. Would you be good enough to make arrangements to have the body, er, dug—"

124

"Exhumed, certainly. I'll hire a couple of men. I suppose you'll want the body in a shroud of some kind?" Fidel nodded. "Please."

"I'll take care of it. Of course you understand that—well, the worst of the decomposition will be over by now, but there will be—a certain amount of—"

Fidel smiled wryly. He was saying that the body would smell to high heaven. That would be fine. Bad smells made good customs inspectors.

"Have you heard from Mrs. Denis?" he asked.

"Yes. She said you'd be bringing back her husband. He was a very fine man; his grave will be waiting. We're all deeply in your debt."

"My pleasure," Fidel said. He had heard the saying somewhere, but it did not sound quite right in these circumstances.

22

FIDEL HAD HALL SEND a message to Gardea, at Villa Camargo. He said he would like a small wagon with two horses, and another span of horses for a wagon he was shipping down.

"Otherwise," he told Tom, "everything's copacetic. I might start a graveyard shuttle service. I could be rich in a year." He grinned.

Hall grimaced. "I told you it was habit-forming! Don't even joke about it. God has no sense of humor."

"He made Frenchmen, didn't he?" Fidel chuckled.

Just before noon, he went into the Palace and

ordered a beer. He drank a schooner without taking a breath, belched, and ordered another. He was a little drunk on all this recent success.

"Tim," he said to the bartender, in his tube-like apron, "that gold bracelet by the Irish whiskey bottle looks familiar."

Tim, the bartender, placed it before him. "Want to buy it? It's for sale."

Fidel hefted it. Its weight was formidable. The eagle on it had a fierce eye of obsidian. "What is that, a bluebird?" he asked.

Tim laughed. "You're full of it, ain't you?" he said. "That is the Mexican eagle. See the rattlesnake in its mouth?"

"That is a worm, Tim. And the bird is still a blue-bird, to me. What are you asking?"

Tim called down the bar: "How much are we asking for this thing of John Hogan's?"

"Fifty. American."

"Sold," Fidel said, digging in his pocket.

Tim shrugged as Fidel worked the split bracelet onto his hairy wrist. "It's none of my business, but it might, you know, make your old partner hear bugles to see you wearing it."

"Oh, I'm not going to wear it," Fidel said. "I'm going to have it cut down for a lady friend. She loves birds, and I think she might like to have this."

"Little heavy for a lady, maybe?" asked Tim, skeptically.

"It'll do," said Fidel. "Till something better comes along."

126

In his hotel room, he wrote on lined paper, in his large script: *"Allie: Where we're going tomorrow it's liable to be pretty hot. You might want to wear short sleeves. I have a bracelet for you that would look beautiful on your wrist."*

The desk clerk sent the message to Allie's for him.

At a jewelry store, he got the goldsmith's promise to cut the bracelet down to a size that would fit a small woman's wrist. It would be ready by closing time.

While he ate at the hotel restaurant, among cattle buyers and mining promoters talking of thousands, he made penciled calculations in tens of dollars. So much for the coffin. So much for the Mexican railroad people. So much for Señor Gardea. So much for the churches, in two countries. So much for ammunition. And a large sum for incidentals. He was beginning to feel poor. But in some canyon near La Barranca, or La Ventana, all of a sudden he would get rich.

Inside he felt excited and trembly, but full of power.

He paid for his meal and walked to the bank. A talk with Leo Lucas might be a good idea, about this hog-commerce plan of Arthur's. Why not? He liked pork, himself. Everybody used candles and soap. Hell, it might be a winner.

Lucas's office was delineated by a half-height wall, and green velour curtains. The door was open, and a very familiar voice drifted out.

". . . My seed money. It's open and shut, Leo. Can't you see that? With a thousand dollars, I can buy seventy-one cows in Mexico. I sell them here—never take them off the cars—for twelve hundred. I pay you the interest and borrow another—what?—eight hundred. This market is going no place but up!"

"John," said the banker, "you don't even have an office now! Nothing to assure me that you'll ever come back. I don't mean that as an accusation. But what kind of a fool would I look like when I told the board I'd made a scary loan like that, and you got lost somewhere? Or robbed? And I had absolutely no collateral?"

"I haven't got robbed yet. And we've always paid back our loans," Hogan argued, with an edge of indignation in his voice.

"We?" said Lucas.

There was a pause. "You think he's so steady, eh? I could tell you—"

Hastily, Fidel tapped the door-frame, glanced inside. "Oh—sorry, Leo. Didn't know you were busy."

Hogan glared at him like an old, battered bull with blood in his eye. "He's not busy," Hogan said. "I was just leaving. But I want to talk to you when you're through here."

"I'm through now. I'm withdrawing a few hundred this afternoon, Leo. I'll need gold. Okay?"

"Of course."

He led the way outside, found a shady spot on the walk and waited. Hogan leaned against the pebbly adobe wall beside him. He pulled a scrap of straw from a mud brick and chewed it with his front teeth.

"I'd say we were at a standoff, pardner," Hogan said, with a grin. When he spoke, he puffed out whiskey fumes.

"How's that?" Fidel said, coldly.

"You ain't going anywhere with Fort Hogan, and I need a good, dumb old uncle like you to keep me out of trouble. What say we try it again?"

"I didn't have much luck keeping you straight before."

"I've had my fling for a while. I'm a new man."

"No," Fidel said.

"Told you you ain't going anyplace with that gun. I mean it."

"I know you mean it. But you can't stop me."

"Like hell I can't. I can tell the customs boys something is coming across."

"And what will that get you? Shot. Someone else is involved in this now."

"Hall? I ain't afraid of that fancy-man gunsmith."

"He ain't afraid of you, either. If you informed, he'd lose some money, and you'd get one right between the ears this time. Sooner or later. Coming home drunk. Sitting drunk leaning in a window. And all for nothing. They'd pay you in corral dust."

"Don't forget the Rurales. Mean bunch of people."

"A mean bunch that know you and I are partners, or think we still are. They'd pay you in rope, John. Or centavos. There's only one way you're going to make any money on this."

Hogan's bleared eyes looked interested, even his left eye opening almost fully.

"Wait till they pay me. Then kill me and steal it. The plan has risks, but everything has. Everything." He poked Hogan with his thumb and walked away.

23

"I USUALLY STAY OVERNIGHT at a mountain village called La Barranca," Fidel told the boarders, at dinner. They were all excited about Allie's intention to travel to Sonora. "The beds are like stone, but at least they're clean. Lice are the curse of Mexico."

"Mr. Fidel—please!" Miss Peacock protested faintly, putting her fingertips to her brow.

"I'm so excited!" Allie said. Her eyes glistening, she looked around the table at everyone—everyone but Fidel. "I've never been farther south than Nogales!"

"The people are friendly," he said. "And you'll feel right at home. All the women are in black from age six on up."

"Actually," Allie said pensively, "I thought I'd wear something else. Without sleeves—cooler, you see for the desert."

"I've got to see that," Hall laughed. "A short-sleeved black shirtwaist?"

"My days of mourning end today," Allie announced. All eating stopped. They stared at her. She still had not looked at Fidel. "Mr. Fidel," she said, "has promised me a bracelet to celebrate the occasion. Isn't that nice of him?"

He was startled. Everyone gazed at him, including

130

Allie, whose eyes were laughing now. He was speechless.

"You didn't forget?" she asked, feigning anxiety.

"No, no! It's right there—in the little box. I was going to surprise you. . . ."

He got up and took a small jeweler's box from the sideboard. He placed it beside her plate and sat down again. Allie opened it, removed the tissue from the bracelet, and held up the bracelet. "It's beautiful!" she cried. Hall stared at it, then at Fidel, and Miss Peacock gasped.

They all knew it from its former life on and off of John Hogan's wrist.

"It's lovely, dear," Miss Peacock murmured. "If it doesn't break your arm."

"Put it on!" Arthur cried.

"Oh, I think I'll wait," Allie said. "You'll all see it at breakfast." She gazed into Fidel's eyes. "Thank you Mr. Fidel. I'll never take it off."

Allie told Miss Peacock she had made arrangements for the general store to deliver fresh food. "And there's something in the ice-box—"

"Now, don't worry about us," Miss Peacock said. "I'm quite capable of feeding our little family. How long will you be gone?"

"Five days, *más o menos,*" Fidel said. "Tom, you can help me at the office, if you aren't busy. Got your replacement lined up? Good. When you pack, Allie, you'd better put in a light-weight jacket of some kind, and a hat for the sun."

"My advice," said Mr. Montana, the druggist, "is the same to people planning a trip to Mexico. Keep your mouth closed and your bowels open. I'll give you some pills to take along."

"Mr. *Montana!*" Allie said, in reproof, then laughed. Miss Peacock left the table with an indignant stare at Montana.

They got to work, blinds drawn, two lamps burning, the door locked. Fidel had carried in some lumber for the work, and the black coffin rested in the middle of the floor. The wagon was parked in the alley for quick loading in the morning.

Six inches above the bottom of the coffin, they nailed one-by-ones around the inside perimeter of the box. Then Hall lined up the ten gun-barrels on the floor, the main shaft beside them, the plates beside the shaft. He laid the drum, wrapped in oily rags, atop the barrels. All the other parts, wrapped, were laid in place, along with boxes of ammunition, tools, and cleaning rods. Broken down, the gun took up little space. Fidel had prepared one-by-sixes to fit, and they placed them over the gun, nailed them down for security, and covered the false floor with the white satin lining O'Brien had provided.

Fidel stood up, massaging his back. "I hope those Indians are good with tools," he said.

"They're as clever as pickpockets. Anyway, I'll assemble it for them, and after that it will only be a matter of cleaning and adjustment."

"Can you say it all in Cáhita?"

"What I can't I can do in sign language."

They closed the coffin, and Fidel sat on it, his head in his hands. "I've got to tell you this. Hogan threatened to tell the customs people I'm bringing it across."

"Does he know?"

"No, but he can guess. I tried to plant in his mind the fact that the gun is worth more to him in the mountains than it is here. If he figures out what I'm doing, he knows I'll be bringing back a load of Mexican gold. So you might want to leave after we deliver the gun."

"Let's take the problems one at a time," Hall said. "Whatever happens, we're making history. The Yaquis have been fighting without artillery or automatic weapons for a couple of hundred years. I'm anxious to see what a single ten-barrel field-piece will do to the course of the war. I might write a paper on it," he added.

"If they reach the Eight Pueblos with it," Fidel agreed, "we'll be reading articles about it in the Mexican newspapers next winter."

And if they didn't, or he didn't reach the rendezvous, that might be regarded as news, too.

24

AT SEVEN O'CLOCK IN the morning the sky already arched hot and clear over the town. Hall and Fidel stood bareheaded in the churchyard, some tools at their feet, while two little boys in red vestments assisted the priest in the exhumation. Nearby, the coffin rested on the caliche earth near the wagon on which it would travel. Juan Arvisu's coffin already showed worm damage as a pair of sweating workmen raised it from the grave. Fidel noticed with approval that it did not seem particularly heavy. He had heard that a month-old corpse lost half its weight; he hoped so. The coffin weighed nearly two hundred pounds empty.

Finishing the ceremonial incantations, the priest made a final sign of the cross, the little boys trotted into the church with the coins Fidel had given them, and the workmen asked whether they should open the coffin now.

"Let's get at it," Fidel said grimly, handing one of them a nail-puller.

He paid the priest and the priest handed him the burial papers from Juan Arvisu's first interment. He laid over Fidel's arm a gray cotton blanket, folded, which was the shroud in which the dead miner was to be wrapped.

With a squall of rusty nails, the lid came off. Fidel wondered if the fumes of decomposition were poisonous, or merely unpleasant. The workmen backed away, holding handkerchiefs over their faces and making the sign of the cross. Fidel gave them a handful of silver coins. They thanked him and got busy refilling the grave.

Then Fidel pulled a little half-pint bottle of bourbon from his hip pocket and soaked two bandanas in it, one for himself, one for Hall. They tied them over their noses and mouths.

They put on gloves and aligned the coffin beside that in which Arvisu would travel. He looked down on the dead man's face, which was almost black, with the sunken cheeks and eyes of a medieval Christ. "God damn!" Fidel said, hoping the corpse did not come apart when they transferred it. "Ready?"

Hall nodded.

They worked their gloved hands under the corpse, which was dressed in a cheap black suit, and lifted. It was amazingly light, drained of fluids, just a sort of chrysalis from which the butterfly had crawled. Cautiously, both of them making gagging noises as the smell of putrefaction overrode that of bourbon, they laid the remains on the shroud. Fidel had unfolded it only half-way. They pulled the edges together over Arvisu, got a grip on the material, and lifted.

In one motion, the miner was transferred to the new coffin. Instead of covering the face, Fidel left it uncovered. He wanted the customs men to see it and be able to smell the putrefaction that now, suddenly, caused Tom Hall to turn and throw up his breakfast.

That started Fidel, too. He heard the workmen laughing at the door of the church.

. . . They laid the lid on the coffin, but installed only four of the handful of screws which were to hold it down. They might be removing the lid in an hour and it might as well be easy as hard. Fidel beckoned the workmen back.

"Give us a hand with this," he said. "The new box is solid oak. It's heavy."

The four of them, however, lifted it without difficulty. The sturdy little delivery wagon, with the gun-carriage front wheels, rocked slightly. The horses were looking around uneasily. Fidel turned away and breathed for a while, then pulled off his gloves and mask.

"Vámonos," he said.

Hall dropped off at Grand Avenue and headed back to the boarding house. According to plan, he would walk Allie over. Fidel did not want to leave the coffin for one minute. At the station, some baggage handlers helped him move it onto a flat-car, of which he had rented half. Then they removed the wheels of the wagon, lifted the bed and axles onto the flat-car, and afterward piled the wheels onto the flatbed beside the coffin.

At the head of the coffin he placed the copper candelabrum he had bought, and installed some candles, which were already wilting in the heat. It looked ridiculous, but the effect on the customs inspector might be useful. He would laugh inside, and feel a little sorry for Fidel in his ignorance, and if he knew anything about corpses, he would not go poking around.

Hogan's voice said, "Very moving, pardner. How about a couple of verses of *A Mighty Fortress?*" He was sitting on a bench in front of the station, a bottle of beer in his hand. "As in Fortress Hogan," he added, to be sure Fidel got the point.

Fidel shrugged. "Suit yourself," he said.

"What's the joke?" Johnny Hogan asked. "Anybody I know in there?"

"You know as much as I do, or you wouldn't be here," Fidel said. "I'm bringing Allie's husband home. Rather than travel dead-head, I'm getting a hundred pesos to carry a Mexican miner to his widow, in La Ventana."

Hogan laughed. "I knew there was a trade you were born to!" he said. "Ain't you going to wear a black suit?"

"No. Just a black band on my sleeve. Who knows, I might lose a friend down there."

With a tug of anxiety, he saw Allie and Tom approaching, Hall carrying her carpetbag, his own gear, and a couple of rifles. Allie was wearing a light-blue cotton dress and a small-brimmed straw hat. Hogan hooted, finished his beer, and mimed a porter hurrying to help someone with bags. "Yassuh, yassuh!" he chortled. He and Hall lined everything up before the waiting room door.

"Thank you, Mr. Hogan," Allie said coldly. "You needn't wait to see us off."

"No, John has business at the bank," Fidel said.

Hogan stroked his chestnut beard, his eyes merry. "Yes, that's right. But you do look first-rate, Mrs. Denis. I knew if you ever came out of that cocoon, you'd be a butterfly for sure, if not a bird."

"John?" Fidel said, moving toward him.

But Hogan took Allie's left hand and held it so that her gold bracelet was displayed. "Now, that touches my heart, Mrs. Denis. You're wearing the bracelet I made while I was in jail in New Mexico. Cut down, evidently, but still a beauty. I modeled the eagle from a Mexican ten-peso piece I had. I'm not really that artistic, but I think it makes a grand wristbrace, for a man. And I've got to say you carry it well."

Allie looked in appeal at Fidel, tears brimming in her eyes. Fidel looked into Hogan's face without saying a word, and Hogan said,

"Well, *adiós,* people. *Bon voyage,* as Bernard would say." Humming *A Mighty Fortress is Our God*, he walked toward town.

Hall went in and talked to the telegraph operator. After lining everything up on the dock, Fidel spoke to Allie, who was still almost in tears, and settled her on the bench to wait. "Nobody knows but us," he said. "And Hogan, for all his loose tongue, isn't going to mention that secret, if he knows it in the first place. Even he has some idea of how far he can go."

Sitting on the flat-car, he looked at his watch now

138

and then. Oh, God, he thought, Arvisu must be heating up something awful! He'll blow the casket apart!

Far up the line, a train's melodious whistle carried down the valley.

25

THE MIXED TRAIN FOR the port of Guaymas, on the Gulf of California, chugged across the border and paused. Mexican immigration men in gray uniforms entered the car. Fidel spoke to one of them, explaining that he must make arrangements with the customs inspectors. He went down the tracks to where a big bankerish-looking Mexican with pince-nez glasses was gazing in consternation at the coffin, some papers in his hand.

Fidel explained it to him. "If you want, I'll open the casket for you—" He displayed a screwdriver.

The officer wrinkled his nose. *"No importa,"* he said. "The wagon? Are you going to sell it?"

"No, just use it to carry the casket."

"All right!" The inspector waved the papers and walked on to inspect the rest of the freight on the car.

Fidel relaxed, almost dizzy with relief. Would the false bottom be obvious, when it was finally inspected? Were the candles too heavy a touch?

The train pulled out. In the dry heat, it puffed southward along a shallow valley beside the Rio de los Alisos. Wind coming through the open windows buffeted their faces. A gritty dust settled over everything.

139

Allie had brought a lunch, and after a while they began eating sandwiches. The heat curled the bread.

"What time will we get there?" she asked.

"About three. I hope you brought a wrap of some kind. That sun will broil a T-bone in fifteen minutes."

"I did. And how far will we get tonight?"

"To La Barranca. It won't take over a half-hour to rig up the wagon. Gardea will have the horses, and another wagon."

At a distance they saw small villages like Mexican hats on the flat horizon.

Allie dozed off. She had removed her straw boater and laid it on her lap. Her head tilted over on Fidel's shoulder and bounced there as the car jolted along. Hall smiled at Fidel. Fidel sighed.

They stopped once for water and mesquite wood. Workmen shouted in Spanish, and trainmen with iron rods checked the journal boxes.

At a tiny station called Casitas, the train stopped unexpectedly. Fidel knew what was coming; it had happened the other day: A military inspection. Two gray-uniformed soldiers who looked like small boys carrying rifles too big for them entered the car. They appeared ignorant and harmless, but they might be some of the same patrol who had hung Yaquis from the crossarms not long ago. He heard them asking passengers, most of them Mexican, where they were going. He was glad they had brought Winchesters instead of Mexican arms this time.

A soldier who looked Indian, with an almost Oriental face and black hair as coarse as a horse's tail, looked them over.

"Where are you going?" he asked.

"Villa Camargo."

"Let me see your tickets." He scrutinized them—Fidel doubted very much whether he could read—and handed them back. "The rifles."

They pulled them out of their boots and he inspected them. "Ween-chest-air," he said. "American Army?"

"No," Hall said, "just sporting guns."

The soldier shrugged and walked on.

The train resumed its sojourn into Sonora.

Fidel was not particularly relieved to feel the train slowing, hear it whistle, and see the buildings of Villa Camargo sliding by. All it meant that the easy part of the trip was over. He studied Hall's blank features. How would he be in a real scrape? When it came to that, would it be possible to survive one? What if they were entrapped by soldiers while assembling the gun for the Yaquis? If there were a shootout, and a single Mexican soldier escaped, they would never leave the country alive. Their strategy would have to be based on a very old principle, that dead men tell no tales. And how would he feel about killing, or trying to kill, men like the peasant boy who had checked them out at Casitas?

The train had stopped, creaking, smoking, steaming. Allie was as excited as a girl, peering out at the countryside, talking about the mountains, impulsively squeezing his arm once. Christ, what have I gotten her into? he thought bleakly. That *puta* in La Ventana! Without her hunger to see the American widow on her knees, Allie wouldn't be here.

But no Allie, no coffin; no coffin, no Gatling gun.

Señor Gardea greeted them as they dismounted. Fidel saw a wagon and horses beyond the station. He shook the rancher's hand and introduced his friends. Gardea invited them to spend the night at his ranch, but Fidel explained that he had freight, this time, that would not keep. . . .

They bolted the wheels back on the wagon, giving it some extra grease as they slid the hubs over the spindles. Fidel had rigged a double-tree in place and the workmen harnessed the horses.

"Why do you need the other wagon?" the rancher asked, curiously.

"I hope to find some garbanzo peas. The ones we get in Nogales are wormy. I think they might catch on if I could find fresh ones. Also I'm bringing back some ore samples from a couple of mines I'm thinking of investing in."

Gardea had uneasy glances for the coffin, but politely refrained from asking about it. When it came time to load the black box, however, Fidel decided he had better explain.

"This lady's husband was a mining engineer. He died last year in La Ventana. We're going to bring his body home. He was a devout Catholic, and desired above all to be buried in his own churchyard." He sighed. "*Ay de mi, amigo!* Man proposes, God disposes."

Gardea crossed himself. "Señora, my profoundest sympathies. I insist that you spend the night with me on the return trip. I will kill an antelope for our dinner."

"Unfortunately," Fidel said quickly, "Señora Denis will take the stage from La Ventana to the railroad at Cananea, so she won't be coming back. But many thanks."

They lashed a tarp over the coffin, and Hall climbed onto the wagon the Mexican had rented them. Allie joined Fidel on the other. With the sun scorching their backs, they headed up the road to the foothills.

26

BY MID-AFTERNOON THEY were among the mountains, like lumbering elephants, of the lower Sierra Tipic. The wagon jolted, tilted, and swayed, but the coffin, roped down, travelled well, and so far it had not burst from the gases. Allie kept seeing unusual birds—red cardinals, a yellow and black oriole. Was she being self-consciously unselfconscious about the bluebird? he wondered.

In a smoky dusk, after a half-dozen halts, they were in the wide lower end of the barranca from which the village took its name. Allie's face was pink with sunburn, and she looked tired. But she was game, and he liked that. He saw the first goat-pen of the village, a

143

half-mile below the Fröcks' place. Allie discovered a floss like silk on her arm. Her forearms were as pink as her face.

"What's that?" she asked.

"Silk, from the big trees up ahead. There ought to be a market for it. In the fall you can hardly breathe for the silk in the air. Worse than cottonwoods."

"I brought my marriage certificate," Allie said. "I thought the woman might want proof."

"She might, but I'm going to give her enough money that she won't give a damn."

"That's the stuff," Allie said enthusiastically. He smiled at her. Bernard hadn't taught her *that* phrase. She was on the way to becoming American again. They rattled past some houses where he was known for the treats he brought; but the children stood in the yard sucking their thumbs and gazing at them. He waved, but they did not wave back.

"Idiotic soldiers have got them spooky about foreigners," he muttered. "I hope they've left. The blasted lieutenant thinks he's going to be the next president."

In fact, the road was deserted; nor was there anyone on the side-road coming from Ricardo's mine. Hall's tired horses lagged a hundred yards behind.

"What a lot of buzzards," said Allie, the birdwatcher.

Fidel started. "What?"

"Over the big tree. They look like mourners!"

Oh, my God, he thought, suddenly stricken ill. Were they mourning anyone he knew?

144

The horses were reacting, too. He shook the reins. On they rattled past empty-looking houses. Children peeked out of doorways and unglazed windows. And there, at the cantina, seven or eight soldiers were emerging to see who had arrived. Little men, big rifles. A non-com pointed a rifle at them, and yelled, and Fidel stopped the horses.

You son of a bitch, he said under his breath.

The sergeant's uniform looked big enough for John Hogan; but the man's face was drunk enough and mean enough for a full squad. He spoke to the other men and they came to look the wagons over.

"Keep smiling," Fidel told Allie, trying to sound lighthearted. "They look tough, but the only one I worry about is the lieutenant. And I've got him in my pocket."

"I don't see an officer," Allie said.

"He'll be along." He raised his hand to the non-com and shoved his boot against the rasping foot-brake. *"Qu'hubole?"* he called.

"What's your name?" the sergeant demanded. Two of the soldiers climbed onto the back of the wagon.

"You know my name. I was through last week. Where's your commanding officer?"

"He's coming. Get down."

"The lady, too? That wouldn't be very polite, sergeant."

The sergeant wiped his nose. "All right."

The soldiers were throwing off the knots that secured the tarpaulin over the casket. "What are you carrying?" the sergeant asked. "Anything for your Yaqui friends?"

"No. . . ." Fidel turned to watch the soldier raise the tarpaulin.

"Name of God!" the soldier gasped. He jumped from the wagon. His companion followed. Fidel heard a horse jogging on the road.

"One of your own people, coming home to La Ventana," Fidel smiled at the sergeant.

The horseman joined them. It was Lieutenant Lopez, carrying a carbine. The sergeant pointed at the coffin and started explaining.

"Shut up," the officer said. "Get up there and remove the lid. Have you got a screwdriver, gringo?"

Fidel climbed back and unlocked the toolbox bolted to the bed of the wagon. He tossed the sergeant a screwdriver. The man groaned as he began removing the screws. In a few moments he straightened up.

"It's loose, Lieutenant."

The lieutenant stepped from his horse onto the back of the wagon. "Lay the lid aside," he said.

Fidel looked at Allie, who had not stirred. "Maybe," he said, "you'd better get down. . . ."

"No," she murmured. "I'm all right."

Fidel pulled out his bandana and tied it over his mouth and nose. "It's a good idea—the man's been dead a long time, Lieutenant," he said.

Lopez looked into the coffin as the lid was removed. He swallowed, murmured a curse. "Yes, all right. Put it back, Morales," he said. He stepped back into the saddle.

146

"Is something dead, Lieutenant?" Fidel asked, indicating the circling buzzards a quarter-mile ahead.

"We butchered a steer. Are you staying with the Germans again?"

"Yes."

"Go ahead. *Buen apetito,*" Lopez smiled, waving his handkerchief before his face.

". . . What was he talking about?" Allie asked, as they drove on.

"He wanted to be sure we weren't carrying contraband."

"What would he do if he caught someone?"

"Shoot them. They're nervous about Indians. The way we were until Geronimo was tamed. I guess we can't criticize them too much."

"Gary!" There was an odd note in her voice, almost a whimper. She turned toward him, pressed her face against his shoulder and began to weep. He had no idea what she was saying, but he knew it was something important. He stared up the road, and saw what had upset her.

Two men were hanging from a limb of a big tree before the Fröck family's home. Buzzards were roosting in the tree. There was just enough wind to cause the bodies to swing slightly.

27

"YOU COULDN'T EXPECT ME to identify him, Lieutenant," Fidel said. "He hardly looks human. I know the German, of course, by his red shirt."

"He was hiding among the goats when we surrounded the house," Lopez said. "He was carrying this. Can you read it?"

They stood in the road before the Fröck house. Lopez had said he had let the woman and the old man go on to El Rincon, where they had friends. Ricardo Fröck had lied about the Yaqui's being there, so he had had to be hung, too.

The wagons were parked down the road; the men had walked to the scene of the hanging with the officer.

"It's not English or Spanish," Fidel shrugged, looking at the writing in Alejandro's black memorandum book. "I suppose it's Yaqui."

Lopez showed the notebook to Hall, too. He shook his head. "I don't know the language," he said. "I don't even know Apache. Why did they have to be hung?"

"Mexican soldiers were killed every day, farther south. It's a war, hombre! We kill them where we find them. They bring their children up like coyotes, train them to kill without mercy, to torture and steal. They are lice. And anyone who traffics with them is executed as well. How long have you known the German?"

He gazed up at the bound man dangling beside the Yaqui from the branch of the tree. He might have been looking at a coyote pelt on a fence, Fidel thought.

"A year and a half."

"What was your relationship with him?"

"It was a place to sleep and feed my horses," said Fidel. "I paid him for the service."

"Yes, I found some American money in his pocket. What's the other wagon for?"

Fidel told him what he had told Gardea, that he was taking ore samples and chick-peas home. He was a trader and a part-time prospector. He talked matter-of-factly, but there was a sort of silent screaming going on inside his head. I could kill this bastard, he thought. He's careless. We could probably finish off his men. But then we'd never get home alive, and neither would Allie. He was not sure how they were going to get out alive, anyway.

Lopez looked at his nails, which were dirty. He gazed into Hall's eyes again. "Why are you here?" he asked. "You don't look like a muleskinner."

Hall shrugged. "My father used to bring me to La Ventana with him to treat sick people. He was a doctor. I know Father Severo. I came to help with the exhumation, in case there are any problems."

"Your business?"

"Telegrapher."

Lopez put the notebook back in his pocket. "You know, they're more like animals than people," he said in disgust. "I'll find his den somewhere, and I'd be

149

surprised if there's enough in it to feed a child. Fleas, lice, and feces, that's what I'll find. When they don't have enough meat, do you know what they do? They tie a string to a piece of meat, chew it and swallow it, then pull it up and pass it to the next one! Animals," he sneered. "You can camp in the road, where you left the wagons," he added. "I'll have someone bring oats for your horses."

They started back. That was the worst news they had had yet, Fidel realized. The fact that he was allowing them to continue meant that the Lieutenant wanted them to keep travelling, to make their rendezvous with the Yaquis, wherever it was and for whatever purpose. Lopez did not understand it, but he knew they were in Sonora for a reason.

They camped on the extra wagon, after eating some beans and rice Fidel bought from a Mexican family. In the morning they woke to tinkling bells, roosters crowing, and barking dogs. Waking, for Fidel, was like coming out of the ether after a painful operation. What he had brought to pass in this town he could never live down. Because of his urging, and because of a feeling of Ricardo's own for the plight of the Indians, he had acted as a mailbox for Fidel.

And now he was hanging from a tree, along with a dead Yaqui.

Mrs. Fröck and her blind husband—he would find them, if he got out of this alive himself, and make financial restitution, at least. Carrying a bucket of water, he saw Lopez's horse before the cantina, and thought,

At least I'll feel better after I take care of Lopez.

How and when? He didn't know, but he made a *manda* of it, as Bernard had made a *manda* to his saint about his heart. His *manda* was in the name of Ricardo and Alejandro.

They harnessed the horses and pulled out. There was no way to get to La Ventana but by passing the Fröcks', but Allie covered her face with a handkerchief as they passed. Fidel could already smell the bodies.

They reached La Ventana during the siesta hour. The little cafe, the Sonorense, was open. Fidel left a boy to watch the wagons while they ate. They had had no breakfast, and they ate the half-burned, half-raw chicken with good appetite.

"Bernard didn't eat here often, I'll bet," he joked.

Allie smiled pallidly.

"There's a stage out of here tomorrow morning," Fidel said. "It goes north to Cananea, which is a big town—fifteen thousand. You can take the train from there to the main line, and be in Nogales the next morning. I don't like you travelling alone, but it will be better than staying with us."

Allie shook her head. "No, it's my sacred duty—"

"Your sacred duty is to get Señora Denis the Second to sign a paper releasing Bernard's body. That's all. Then you're going home."

"Well, perhaps I should," Allie agreed. "As long as I live, I'll never forget—" She began to cry again.

He patted her hand.

151

After lunch they walked to the church. Father Severo spoke no English, and Allie spoke no Spanish, but they communicated through the Basque. The padre pointed out to her the line Estella Nava must sign before he could let the body be moved. In anticipation of that signing, he told Fidel, he would have the body exhumed and Juan Arvisu buried in the grave Fidel insisted on paying for.

They left the church. People were reappearing on the walks and in the plaza as the siesta wore off. Fidel asked Tom to stay with the wagons while he walked Allie down to Calle de las Reyendas.

"You'd better ask them to wait till I get back to take Arvisu out of the coffin," he said. "I guess he'll have to camp out this time around. Not many of them get coffins anyway."

Fidel tapped at the open door of Estella's home. She materialized from the shadows, yawning. When she saw Allie, fresh but grave in baby blue, she looked shocked. She regarded her with great curiosity, but with much more shyness than he had expected.

"Señora Denis?" Fidel said. "May I present, er, Señora Denis?"

"*Mucho placer,*" murmured Estella.

"*Mucho placer,*" Allie said quickly, in a hushed voice, and smiled shyly. "I have a paper—Doesn't she speak any English?" she asked Fidel, in distress.

"Of course not. I'll explain it." As he began speaking, his fingers worked with three goldpieces, like Johnny Hogan debating a bet. The Mexican woman stared at the coins. To her, he knew, they were a couple of months' earnings, at least.

"Padre Severo says you'll have to sign here, where it's checked. Then he can release the remains."

Docilely, Estella nodded. "You'll have to write my name, and I'll make my X," she said.

Fidel had an indelible pencil. Using the chest of drawers for a desk, he wrote the woman's name with care, adding, *"Her mark."* Then Bernard's second widow drew an X. Fidel wondered how many widows he had left in France and other countries! He placed the coins on the dresser, and smiled at her. She unfastened the necklace and amulet, and handed them to Allie.

"I'll have some prayers said for you," said Fidel.

"No, no! For Bernardo, in my name. And some candles, for Santa Felicitas."

"Adiós, señora," Fidel said.

"Adiós. Adiós, señora," Estella replied.

On some impulse, Allie gave her an *abrazo.* Then she pulled up her bracelet to disclose the bluebird on her wrist. Estella stared, then smiled and nodded. Allie pushed the bracelet down to her hand again, smiled, and they left.

"Why did you do that?" asked Fidel, in anguish.

"So she would understand."

"Understand what?"

"That I wasn't condemning her. That I understood. And so she wouldn't condemn me. Maybe the feel-

153

ings we have towards other people are totaled some-where. . . . You can't be too careful about how you treat people."

Just before sunset, in the high-walled *campo santo,* Juan Arvisu was laid to rest. Fidel had paid two years' rent on his plot. The widow, to his relief, had not appeared. Then Bernard Denis was wrapped in a shroud and placed in the coffin. Allie waited in the church, a handkerchief over her head, since she was not in black. The coffin was carried into the church to spend the night. Fidel thanked the priest, signed a paper, and rejoined the others. The horses were sta-bled, and they found rooms in the almost empty, echoing Hotel La Posta.

Fidel went out to buy a bottle of rum, and saw three men at the hitchrack of the hotel. One, who wore a Stetson with gold braid, was saying in English to another, a Mexican:

"Let's just leave them right here. You never know when you'll need a horse. Go up to the stable, Ruben, and buy them some oats. Have a *mozo* bring some water. We'll keep the saddles in our rooms— Well, hello, *compadre!*" Johnny Hogan exclaimed, seeing Fidel.

"A little off the reservation, John?" Fidel said.

"Out beatin' the bushes for cattle," Hogan replied, removing and replacing his hat. "Gardea's talking cash now, and I'm short as usual."

"So you're hoping to get well quick, right?"

Johnny spread his hands. "One man's loss is another man's gain. You just have to keep trying, Fidel."

"That sounds like a sermon, John. But you don't impress me as a preacher, somehow. When I look at you, I see something more like what I saw in La Barranca today. You've got the smell on you."

Chet Hardin, red-faced and exhausted, was trying to appear ready for anything. He did this by resting his hand on his hip near the Colt he carried.

"I don't have an enemy in the world," Hogan said.

"Keep thinking that," Fidel said. "If the situation changes, I'll let you know."

He walked on to a cantina. He knew he was safe in La Ventana, now, because Hogan was following him. Lopez did not want him killed.

Allie went to her room early. She would leave at eight A.M. on the stagecoach. Fidel and Tom shared a room down the tiled hall, drinking the rum he had found.

"At least we got her out of it," he said gloomily. "If I didn't need you to assemble and adjust the gun, I'd send you back too. Of course, you can still back out. So can I. But I want to do something for those people."

"I've been coming down here for fifteen years," Hall said. "That isn't the first atrocity I've seen. And Lopez isn't the first banty rooster officer I've wanted to kill."

Fidel poured two drinks and lay on a cot, the straw pallet crackling under him. "We've got a new

155

problem, now," he said. "Hogan and his men are in town. I just talked to them."

"You expected it, didn't you? But old John doesn't want action, he wants gold."

"I don't think you get the picture. After we deliver the gun, we're going to have the gold. That's where John's figuring starts. Then the problem will be to separate us from it. That shouldn't be too hard."

"It doesn't sound too easy, either. Are the soldiers going to let him carry it off?"

"If the soldiers finish us off along with the Yaquis, what happens? He's got a coffin on a wagon. Why would Lopez want it? He might even think John was sincere about delivering Bernard to a cemetery somewhere. So he'd let him take it. Hell, John might even do it! But he'd be damned sure to search the coffin before he delivered Bernardo to his reward."

He sipped some rum. "What I'm counting on is the fact that if Lopez has a man here in town, so have the Yaquis. They haven't survived hundreds of years by being dumb. We may not have a plan, but I'll bet they do."

"It's going to have to be one that will make Alexander the Great look like a raw recruit," Hall said.

28

IN THE MORNING FIDEL looked out the window over the plaza, scratching his ribs. The early morning air was sweet and clear, with smoke rising here and there in straight columns among the hills. Suddenly he heard swearing below the window, in American and Spanish, and leaned out to see what was going on.

"My God!" he said, turning toward Hall, who was shaving. "You'll have to see this."

They gazed down at a group of men, Mexican and American, surrounding three horses lying in a tangle before the hitchrack. John Hogan was there, and his hired hands. They were staring at the horses, who were motionless. A small lake of blood had puddled on the ground near the hitchrack.

"Some sonofabich shot these horses!" Hogan's voice suddenly roared, and he stared quickly at the upper windows of the hotel.

Fidel saluted him. "Impossible, John," he called down. "You didn't hear any shots, did you?"

"No, but you've got eyes, ain't you?"

"Yes, and they look dead, all right. But if you don't have any enemies, who'd cut their throats? There's a big vein that you can cut, you know—doesn't hurt the horse more than the bite of a horsefly. He just quietly bleeds to death. But who would do a thing like that?"

"If I thought it was you—!" Hogan called back.

"I'm not stupid, John. You'd just rent more horses.

Whoever did it must have been trying to tell you something. Better get those carcasses moved. The stage will be pulling up there in a half-hour."

They went downstairs to wait for Allie to appear. She had her carpetbag with her when she did so. Hogan came striding out, carrying his saddle, but he did not speak. He carried a Winchester, as though he were going to war. Fidel had seen the horses dragged away a few minutes ago. In a short time they heard a bugle blow.

"That's the stage," he said. "Now, listen, Allie. You've got to eat, but be careful. Stick with chicken and rice. Don't eat any sour beans, and stay away from milk."

Allie smiled faintly, and reached up to settle her little straw hat. "And avoid strangers?" she asked.

"At least try. Tonight, in Cananea, stay at the Azteca."

He heard the stage rolling up before the hotel, and Hall picked up her bag and carried it out. Fidel had not seen her smile since La Barranca, and he sensed that she was close to tears.

"Say something that will reassure me," she pleaded.

"There's nothing to worry about," he promised her. "The Indians don't bother stagecoaches in this area."

"I'm not worried about myself—I'm worried about you. I don't know what you're up to, but don't ever do it again. Get it over with, and then come home."

"What happened yesterday won't happen again. I'm just bringing Bernard home, and who'd steal a coffin?"

"Yes, that sounds reasonable," Allie agreed. "I just don't happen to think it's all you're doing. Kiss me goodbye."

Fidel held her in his arms and felt her shiver. Then he walked her out. The stagecoach was filling with passengers, and handlers were cramming the last bags into the luggage boots. A guard with a shotgun climbed up beside the driver. Fidel kissed her again, and helped her into the coach. The whip popped, the mules lunged into the collars. The stage rolled down the street to the Cananea road.

He wished he were on it.

In the hotel room, he got out a wrinkled government map of the La Ventana area. Hall, who knew map reading from the army, pored over it. If the contact with the Yaquis were going to be made between here and El Rincon, it would have to be done in one of the small canyons along the way. The main road followed a deep canyon that twisted through the mountains. They discussed the various barrancas and canyons indicated by the contour map.

Hall's finger traced one of them. "There's one it *won't* be," he said. "Cañon de la Amboscada— Ambush Canyon."

The contours revealed that the canyon wound a half-mile from the main barranca before being crushed among steep cliffs. He supposed a patrol—Spanish, Mexican, Indian—had at some time been trapped in the canyon, and given it its name. But Yaquis did not let themselves get trapped.

What they were looking for was a canyon or wash that led up to high ground and a little-used trail. "There's one," Hall said. "Los Hornitos. Old trails all over, and a spring—Do you know the area?"

"Well, I've passed it. It's about two hours from here. A dry meadow on the left. Sounds likely. Only one thing."

Hall looked at him.

"Yaquis avoid likely places. I've met them in the damndest spots you can imagine. But this time they'll have a gun-carnage to drag, so they're going to have to use a trail."

"We'd better get started. I've got to do my work in good light. Then we ought to get as far back down the hill as we can. We can't go through La Barranca, or Lopez is going to want to know what happened to our other wagon."

But Fidel knew, and Hall must know, that the patrol would not be in La Barranca today. Lopez would be following them, possibly with Hogan as his blood-hound.

With help, they loaded the coffin onto the smaller wagon. Father Severo blessed it, and they headed down the street to the El Rincon road.

For the first half-hour they were among worked-out

mines where men and women labored among the big stone basins called arrastras. Stones tied to cross-arms were dragged around and around by workmen or burros, pulverizing ore. The road followed small canyons among rough hills. In a good day's drive, you could reach the railroad.

Fidel, leading, drove the small wagon. His nerves were jangled, and to settle them he kept taking deep breaths. He watched for the slightest movement in the brush or trees.

If I were Lopez, he thought, what would I do? I would let the Americans go, but keep an eye on them. Lopez had already inspected the coffin and decided it was what it appeared to be. So why stop them again? But sooner or later, he would reason, the Americans were going to make contact with the Indians. And he would be there not long after, and catch them red-handed.

He read the map and tried to relate what he read to what he saw. A certain spring; a stone corral; an Indian cave. No, it was not possible to make the switch! If they stopped long enough to set up the gun, to hide the money under the body of the Frenchman, they would be caught. It was idiocy to think they could do it.

There was only one way out, now: to give up, drive on to the railroad, take the gun back. And perhaps try it again some day. He heard Hall whistle, and pulled up.

Hall was gesturing toward the road behind him. "Think I saw somebody!" he called.

Fidel grimaced. If those fools get close enough, he decided, we might as well settle the score with them and worry about it later.

He shook the horses up a little as he drove on. Not that he could possibly lose those bloodhounds. In a short time they passed a ruined adobe house on the right. The barranca called Ambush Canyon was not far ahead.

How would you explain to a Yaqui soldier, he wondered, that you had a Gatling gun in the box, but had decided not to sell it?

A little park opened up before him, a gully emptying into the deep barranca they were following. The gully came in on the left, and, if he remembered correctly, it was the one called Ambush Canyon. He looked back. Hall was hunched over, his face grim. He had drawn his rifle and laid it on the seat beside him.

A pebble clattered against the side of the wagon. He thought it might have been thrown up by the hoof of one of the horses. But then another pebble struck the floorboards, and he turned his head. Two men in dark clothing were standing in the brush. They wore the hand-woven *jipi* straw hats of Yaqui soldiers, and one man was beckoning them into the mouth of the narrow canyon.

29

FIDEL ACKNOWLEDGED THE MAN'S gesture, but drew his rifle, jumped down, and ran to where the soldiers waited. They had the burnt-wood features of the Yaqui Indian, the flat Oriental eyes. The older man wore a mustache. Fidel began talking in Spanish, almost babbling.

"We can't do it. Alejandro was executed yesterday! We're being followed."

"I know, hombre. How many soldiers?"

"Three Americans, and maybe a dozen Mexican soldiers. I don't know. But I'm certain we don't have time."

"Where is the gun?"

"In the coffin, under a dead man. If we try it, we'll all be dead men."

"Is the other man the gunsmith?"

"Yes." Fidel felt as though he were sinking into quicksand. He was determined to go ahead! Damn! "But there isn't time! It would take—who knows?—maybe a half-hour to assemble the gun."

"Drive up the canyon! *Apúrete!* We've moved the rocks so that you can reach the upper end of it."

"If we reach it," Fidel argued, "how will we ever get out? Aren't the walls steep?"

The Yaqui gestured impatiently. "You're wasting time. Turn the horses."

Fidel trotted back to the wagon and climbed to the

163

seat, babbling to himself. He turned the team into the narrow gully, and the younger Indian came to take his off horse by the headstall and lead it up the trail. The other man ran back and climbed up beside Tom Hall. They began talking earnestly in Cáhita.

As they drove, brush rasping against both sides of the wagon, Fidel asked the man who was leading the horses:

"How many of you are there?"

"Enough," the man said.

"Is he the gunsmith?"

"Yes—Ignacio. Though I know guns, too. We'll all know this gun in a few days."

The canyon walls grew more sheer, of red sandstone, and there was less brush. What was happening was that they were following a gully cut into the earth by the runoff of summer rains. It had been going on for so long that the defile was now chiselled narrow and deep, and there was simply no way to climb out of it. Where was all that Yaqui savvy he had heard about?

He heard a gunshot behind them. Then voices, shouting in panic. Then silence again.

"What was that?" he asked the Yaqui.

"One of the men who was following has died."

"Do you have many men on the hillsides?"

"No. We don't need many. How many *yoris* can come through this canyon at one time? It gets so narrow, ahead, that we'll have to leave the other wagon behind. We may even have to leave this one, and carry the dead-box."

The canyon walls grew more sheer, the brush thinned, the winding passage was almost too narrow for the wagon. He tried to understand their strategy. Get themselves in a position where only a couple of soldiers could come at them at a time, knock them off as they came. But in time, a day or so, soldiers could certainly surround this little canyon and pour a fire on them from above. Or, if that were not feasible, they could simply sit down and wait for them to come out.

So what the hell were they thinking of?

"What's your name, friend?" he asked. "I like to know the people I'm going to die with."

"Paco," the Yaqui said.

"Are you a fox soldier?" He knew it was an honor to be a fox soldier, that it had some religious significance.

"Yes."

"Aren't fox soldiers supposed to be smarter then the *yoris?*"

"Of course!" The Yaqui sounded indignant.

"Then what the hell are we doing in a place called Ambush Canyon?"

The Yaqui murmured something that translated to, None of your business.

Almost without warning the wagon hubs grated against the sandstone walls of the barranca, and the wagon was halted. There was a glimpse of a clearing ahead. The horses strained, but he held them.

"Far as we go, Paco," Fidel said. "Let me explain something. The front wheels, and the tongue, are the carriage of the gun I'm carrying. We'll have to lift the wagon and pull the wheels forward. If you want to try to rig up the field-piece, that is."

The other wagon halted just behind them, and the two Yaqui soldiers shouted back and forth. Another Yaqui appeared in the pass ahead of them. He wore a red headband and a black shirt with small yellow polka dots, and carried a bolt action Mauser. They told him what they had been discussing. Fidel peered hopefully ahead, praying to see a couple of dozen Yaqui soldiers; but it looked as though this was going to be it.

Five of them against God knew how many Mexicans, and a couple of Americans.

Goodbye, Allie. *Adiós,* Great Western Trading Company!

30

THE OLDER MAN IN the red headband was called Manolo, and he was in charge. The gunsmith, who had ridden with Tom, was Ignacio. While they chattered, in Spanish and Cáhita, Fidel got busy with the job of breaking loose the kingbolt so that the wagon could be lifted off the front axle. He had leaned his Winchester against the sandstone wall a few feet from where he worked.

The Indians were hauling the coffin forward, over the seat of the wagon, the only way it could be moved ahead. They lowered it to the ground, carried it a few

166

yards away, and all got their shoulders under the bed of the wagon to lift. As soon as the kingbolt pulled loose, Fidel urged the horses forward, and they pulled the front wheels and axle into the clearing he had seen ahead.

It was small. From the hard earth grew a few twisted ironwood shrubs, a half-dozen small trees, and some graze that would have depressed a goat. The clearing was a pear-shaped bowl that opened up just beyond the narrows; a perfect corral, but a terrible place for a last stand. They carried the coffin a few dozen yards into the clearing and set it down against a sandstone wall.

Hall was giving orders. Lay the tarp there. Open the dead-box and move the corpse out of the way. There's a sack under the false bottom, put the boxes of shells in it. Don't lay the drum in the dirt, keep it clean!

Manolo spoke to Ignacio, who remained at Hall's side, listening to everything he said. Then the two remaining Yaquis went over to where the wagon, tilted down now like a child's slide, completely blocked the pass. They took up positions behind it.

A moment later a bullet ripped white splinters from the wagon, and a triple crash of gunfire banged and echoed in the canyon. Manolo rose just high enough to fire over the wagon, emptying his twelve-shot Mauser down the canyon. Then he moved aside and began reloading from his bandoliers.

Paco took a turn at firing. When he was through, Fidel moved into position. He was anxious to see what was ahead. There was some cautious return fire. He waited until it ceased before glancing over the wagon. All he could see was the narrow defile, smudged now with powdersmoke. He held his fire and looked back at the gunsmiths. Hall had already begun to assemble the rifle barrels on the crank shaft, the front and rear plates securing them in place. Ignacio watched him, nodding. And this goes here, and that goes there, Fidel thought bitterly. And then you turn two Americans loose to try to find their way home.

Even if they killed all but one of the men who had them bottled up here, that would be enough to condemn them. Well, if there were a choice, he'd prefer to die beside a Yaqui, rather than be hung from a tree.

There came another splintering salvo of firing from down the canyon, closer this time, probably from behind the other wagon. He looked and saw that both of Hall's horses were down and the wagon almost filled the gap. He waited for the firing to ease off, and looked for a target. Behind the wagon he saw a face he knew, like a visage in a nightmare, smoke-veiled; it was Hardin, the boozing cowboy, and he took a bead on it and fired.

The Winchester had a kick like a sledgehammer; he remembered the sweet little kick of the Mauser that night. He wondered which American had been killed by that first shot they had heard. Johnny? He hoped so. He would hate to think that John Hogan outlived Gary Fidel, if only because Johnny had predicted that he would die a gun-smuggler's death.

Small consolation.

He looked back to where Hall, the happy gunsmith, was assembling the firing mechanisms. Son of a gun looks like he enjoys it. Well, it's a good way to go as any, he thought, die doing what you do well. The hopper goes here, Ignacio. Catch on? The hinge slides in like this. Then the drum can be fitted on top of the hopper; but that will be later.

After the Mexicans recover it, Fidel thought wryly.

More firing now, sounding much more distant. One thing was as clear as spring water: Lieutenant Lopez and his troops were among those present. Two Americans with Winchesters could not be making all that noise.

Something else bothered him, too.

"I don't see much point," he said to Manolo, the general of this little expedition, "in exposing ourselves this way. Why don't we back off, and just pick off anybody that comes over the wagon, like nits? We've got plenty of ammunition—there's hundreds of rounds for the Gatling gun, that we won't be needing. But if we keep peeking over this wagon bed, we're going to start taking some casualties. And if I've counted right, there's only five of us."

"You haven't counted right," Manolo said tersely. But he agreed that they should move back and take up positions behind rocks, leaving Ignacio and Tom to work on the gun.

Fidel selected a point from which he could see not only the passageway, but his partner working on the gun. It actually began to look like a gun, now. The barrels were installed in the casing, there was a plate with a knob on it at the breech end, and another plate at the muzzle end from which ten forty-five caliber barrels protruded. And the whole thing rested on the carriage, now. It looked wicked.

Wouldn't it be wonderful if he got Fort Hogan firing?

No, because the Mexicans would take one salvo from it, back off, and starve them out.

He could see its working no other way.

Anyway, Allie, he thought with wry contentment, I got here. Hogan said I was too dumb to take chances and make money. I guess I showed him. I hope he was the one they got, because otherwise he might be bringing my money home.

Now it was very quiet, but down-canyon they were moving. He could hear suspicious sounds. Yet there was no firing. Lopez's men were moving in on them. Had Fidel's strategy been faulty after all? Perhaps they had to risk casualties to inflict them.

More shooting broke out, and some swearing identifiable as American. Manolo and Paco exchanged comments from their vantage points. Manolo called something to Ignacio, who yelled back, excitedly.

Then the rush came.

Owl-eyed Ruben Lara, who had guts as well as good vision, dived over the wagon-bed and landed on the ground at its base. A Yaqui shot him in the head. Then Johnny Hogan came sprawling into view, landed and began crawling toward a rock. Fidel pursed his lips and took aim, "Hey, John!" he yelled. He saw Hogan's bearded face for a moment, and if he did not look happy, he did not look scared, either. Too bad you were crazy, John, he thought, as he squeezed off the shot.

"Here they come!" Hall shouted. There was a babble of voices, screams, shots, and a wave of Mexican soldiers came scrambling over the wagon. They're crazy! They're crazy! Fidel yelled, or thought he yelled.

"Didn't they tell you?" Hall screamed back at him, "There's a cork in the bottle! There's fox soldiers down the canyon that came in behind us after the Mexicans closed in on us. That's what they're running from. Watch this bastard fire now, man!"

Hall turned the side-crank of the gun as though he were making ice-cream. The gun blazed and roared. Fidel had never seen anything like it. The Gatling gun held perfectly steady, merely jerking a bit. It smoked like a forge and spat little jets of flame. Arching shells glittered in the sunlight as they were ejected. The top edge of the wagon was torn to shreds. The noise was so shattering that Fidel's ears hurt.

The gun went silent. Hall was still hunched beside it, apparently waiting; so there was nothing wrong with the piece. Fidel's numbed ears recorded, faintly, other shouts, and screams. They were coming closer, but Hall held off until he saw men crawling up to the wagon. Then he began firing again, in bursts.

Fidel was dazed, stunned, deafened. There was now so much smoke in the little bowl that you could hardly see the bullet-shredded wagon. He tried to count the number of bodies on the ground, and thought there were over a dozen. And behind the wagon there were still more.

He heard Yaqui voices beyond the barricade, and the soldiers near him stood up. *"Es todo,"* Manolo said to him.

That's all. That's it.

"No survivors?" Fidel asked hopefully. "Didn't any of them get away?"

"No. We couldn't let them. We need a headstart, too. We'll talk about the money, now."

Fidel gestured with both hands, like a man trying to make a foreigner understand him. He felt like a man taking a part in a play. He was floating high as a vulture, but when he came down he would be so tired they might as well bury him.

"The money, right," he said, hardly able to hear his own voice over the ringing in his ears. "Four saddle-bags of gold, Alejandro said. We'll put it in the coffin, where the gun was. And put Señor Denis over the gold, and then get that other wagon backed out. I'll need the horses, though. Can I have them?"

"We've got horses," Manolo said. "And now we've got a gun. If you ever come to the Yaqui River, we'll induct you into the fox soldiers."

"Thanks," Fidel said. "It may not be for a while, though."

31

IN THE CURTAINED OFFICE, Fidel and Hall counted Mexican goldpieces, making them into little stacks of ten, like John Hogan gambling. The coffin, on a rented wagon, was parked in the dark alley behind the building. Hall had two thousand dollars coming, according to the deal Fidel had made him that day on the street. They finished counting, and the total was only a few hundred dollars off. Fidel put Hall's share in a canvas bag. They had returned on the train two hours ago.

"It would be a pity to let money like that lie around in a bank," he said. "You could put two thousand with this and own half of Great Western."

"Are you really going back?" Hall asked.

"It's my trade, Tom. Fidel the Trader—nice old-world sound, hasn't it? Allie'd like it. But to run guns again? No, thanks. If I'm lucky, nobody but Lopez suspected me, aside from his men, and nobody's going to convict me on their testimony. Diversify—that's what Arthur keeps telling me. And I mean to."

Hall pulled a handful of newly-minted goldpieces from the bag and looked at them as though they could tell him which way to jump. "How often would you say this sort of thing happens?" he asked. "I've been helping you for about three weeks, and I've already been in two military actions. Would you say once a week? Once or twice a year?"

"Never again. I've put some money down on that rendering plant Arthur scared up. He'll run it for me, at least on paper. Then I was thinking about that cock-and-bull story I was telling Lopez—that I was importing garbanzo peas. It might be a winner. The Mexicans love them. Any I can't sell over here, I can sell across the line. And of course the mining supplies thing runs itself—"

"Yes, I noticed," Hall said. "Well, I'm too tired to argue. Why not? But what about—?" He jerked a thumb toward the alley.

"I'll get Father Abelardo to do the honors. I hate to see Allie in black again, dammit, but I guess it can't be helped. But after the funeral, I'll burn all her black dresses."

"Do you feel all right?" Hall asked, noticing him rubbing his brow.

"Oh, sure. Little tired. Hot in here, isn't it?"

As it turned out, Fidel was too sick to attend the funeral. An unusual fever brought him down that night. He sweated until he had soaked the sheets, and had guilty nightmares about corpses kicking at the ends of ropes. In the morning a maid came to his room to remind him that it was time to go to the funeral. Someone had telephoned. Fidel stared at her, thinking he knew her, but that she was dressed differently.

"Where's your blue dress, Allie?" he asked.

"I have no blue dress, señor. I am Luz, the maid. I will tell the manager."

"No! Don't tell him anything!" Fidel croaked.

174

"Lieutenant Lopez is a liar. He— he'll—" Then he looked dully around the room, trying to remember it. He had thought he was back in the cantina at La Barranca; someone was warning him that Lopez was coming with a rope and a squad of riflemen.

After the funeral Allie visited him, wearing black, all right, but with a tuft of pink desert flowers in her hat. She brought him some water, and a tube of pills from Dr. Hall's medicine case.

"I used to give these to Tom's father," she said. "They'll bring a fever down. Though I think you may have it coming to you."

She sat primly beside the bed, her knees together and a prayer book in her hands. She had left the door open.

"What did I do, Allie?" Fidel panted.

"I don't know. Do you want to confess to me? There's an odor I used to notice on my husband's clothes when he'd been in the tunnel after they'd blasted. I suppose it was powdersmoke. The clothes on that chair reek of it. The whole room."

Fidel closed his eyes. He was too sick to argue. "That's what it is. We stopped at a mine after we left you. I got an order."

Allie shook her head in disbelief. "I'll give you another order," she said, rising. "Eat the soup I send down. If I had a spare room, I'd move you in. But for the time being, I'll send your meals down. Nothing but soup. And don't cheat. I've already lost one man to the mines, Gary, and I don't want to lose another. Behave yourself."

"That's good advice," Fidel said, reaching for her hand. It felt icy. She squeezed his fingers briefly, then pulled down the shade and went out, closing the door quietly.

Fidel sighed deeply, felt numbness rising in him like water in a well, and drowned in it, blissfully.

Center Point Publishing
600 Brooks Road • PO Box 1
Thorndike ME 04986-0001 USA

(207) 568-3717

US & Canada:
1 800 929-9108